THE KING IN YELLOW

THE KING IN YELLOW

THOM RYNG

ARMITAGE HOUSE
SEATTLE
2006

EDITIO VULGATA

Text copyright © 1999, 2006 Thom Ryng.

Introduction copyright © 2004 John Tynes.

Cover art copyright © 2004 Jacqueline Brasfield.

All rights reserved worldwide.

This play is the sole property of the author and is fully protected by copyright. It may not be acted by professionals or amateurs without written permission and the payment of a royalty. All rights, including professional, amateur, stock, radio and television, motion picture, recitation, and public reading are reserved. All inquiries should be addressed to the author at: cherryblossomking@gmail.com.

ARMITAGE HOUSE

Published by Armitage House
5536 25th Ave. NE
Seattle, WA 98105-2415
www.tccorp.com

First Hardcover Edition, Limited to 500 signed copies : February 2000 (Editio Princeps).

First Trade Paperback Edition: March 2006.

ISBN: 1-4116-8576-8
ISBN13: 978-1-4116-8576-5

Printed in the United States of America.

Contents

Introduction vii
Forward to the Second Edition ix
Forward to the First Edition x
Acknowledgements xii
Cast of the 1999 Production xiii
Dramatis Personæ: xiv

THE KING IN YELLOW
Prologue 3
Act I, Scene i 7
Act I, Scene ii 33
Act II, Scene i 57
Act II, Scene ii 73
The Unseeing Eye 97

Introduction

THE ENVELOPE held two tickets, emblazoned with the Yellow Sign. This was an ominous event.

The instructions directed us to drive two hours south to a town we had never been before, where we were to attend a dress rehearsal of a particular play. We drove. The play was in a crumbling old theatre, unsafe to enter, a piss-bum of a proscenium.

The cast was aghast. No one was expected to respond to the missive. We were seated hurriedly and with stammer.

Behind us, as we waited for the play to begin, we noticed: a figure in white, all in white, top of head to tip of toe, seated there, quiet, still. Had it been there from the first? We were unsure. Now it looked like a corpse wrapped, moments before the brain was extracted through the nose and the oils and spices bound into the casing.

We whispered. We craned our heads around to behold the specter. We fidgeted.

The figure coughed.

We did not look. We did not spin round. But we were electric, fear and dread, delicious like butter on bread.

One of us had a gun. I should explain. Before we entered the theatre, we cased the joint. Front and back, alleys and exits. If trouble ensued. We knew. We knew how to get out.

We had a gun. A compact revolver, palm-sized, with a flush hammer so it would not catch on the lining of your pocket when you pulled it out. We were taking no chances.

The figure coughed. It was alive. This thing seated behind us in the crumbling red velvet seats, it coughed or choked or perhaps swallowed a particularly toothsome bit of child.

The play started. The figure rose. It strode forward to the stage. Events unfolded.

The first act ended. We reeled. Silence fell. The playwright took the stage.

"Today we are only doing act one. We will perform the rest of the play on opening night."

We had a gun. We knew how to use it. We almost drilled a

hole in his heart on the spot. The world would not miss a playwright.

Come back? Was he serious? To see the special second act which they would only perform with a full audience of eager victims? Was the man mad?

We almost drilled a hole in his heart on the spot.

Instead we left. Instead we came back. We saw the full play. The world did not end. No one was harmed in the making of theatre.

Now that playwright, Thom, whose life we spared only out of cowardice and a sad dereliction of duty, is a trusted friend, a fellow traveler. This is indisputable. I have helped him move.

Still I think: did we do the right thing? That day? When we did not drill a hole through his heart? And then: was it wise to compound our error of mercy by publishing his book, giving him access to a wider audience?

Questions are a burden to others. Answers are a prison to oneself. The walking shadow walks on, struts and frets, and then all is darkness. Curtain.

Bang.

John Tynes
Seattle, Washington
November 2004

Forward to the Second Edition

And now, far away, over leagues of tossing cloud-waves, I saw the moon, dripping with spray; and beyond, the towers of Carcosa rose behind the moon. (Robert W. Chambers, "In the Court of the Dragon")

AS I WRITE THIS, almost seven years have passed since *The King in Yellow* premiered on the stage. And what years they have been! Seven years ago who could have imagined a Department of Homeland Security? The parallels between the play and our unfolding times are eerie to some, but people have been playing chess in burning houses throughout human history, and there is no reason to suppose they will ever stop.

When the first edition came out, the publisher and I agreed to a bit of fun. My name appeared only as the translator, and the book claimed to be a new version of the "original" play. It's all a fiction of course: like H.P. Lovecraft's *Necronomicon*, Robert Chambers' *The King in Yellow* play is only a plot device. At least, that's how it started.

This is not *The King in Yellow*. Right now, someone else is writing the True Version. What you hold in your hand was the True Version once, as were those of Lin Carter and James Blish and who knows how many others in their turn. I have personally collected seven versions so far, and I'm confident there are others that have (for the moment) escaped my scrutiny. There is no great magick here, no spell except the more usual sort that every author hopes to cast. Every supposed consequence is coincidence, easily explained.

Even the well-timed transiting of the Hyades over the horizon as seen from the epicenter of the Nisqually Earthquake. Truly.

Tacoma, Washington
February 2006

Forward to the First Edition

One does not become enlightened by imagining figures of light, but by making the darkness conscious. (C.G. Jung)

LE ROI EN JAUNE was written in 1890 by an anonymous French playwright and published later that year. The play and its author were quickly denounced by the Church, and the play was banned by the Paris authorities and suppressed by the police in 1891. So far as is known, it was never performed in the original French. Subsequent English editions appeared under the title *The King in Yellow* in London and Edinburgh in 1892, and at Chicago's Columbian Exposition of 1893. Rumours abound that the anonymous author committed suicide, though a reviewer of the time opined that "bullets couldn't kill a fiend like that."

The play is known today chiefly through the writings of the American author Robert W. Chambers, who in 1895 published a short story collection also titled *The King in Yellow*. Chambers based his stories upon the lives of some of those touched by the play, for the play reportedly had a queer effect indeed on those who read it in the first years of its release. They were infected with a kind of shared, delusional reality perhaps best exemplified in Chambers' story "The Repairer of Reputations." Simply, the objective cosmos that was taken for granted in Victorian times was replaced by a series of overlapping subjective realities, each more irrational than the last. Gradually, a kind of disconnect between these various "truths" developed, resulting in emotional stress and, in the worst cases, psychosis. The play was terrifying, not because it contained any great evil, but rather because, prefiguring the surrealists and post-modernists of our own time, it exposed Truth as a phantom and, anticipating Lovecraft, it revealed the essential hopelessness of man's search for meaning in a cold and dispassionate universe.

Although Chambers' book has been in print for much of the past century, no English edition of the play itself has appeared since 1893. In 1995, I undertook a new translation, working from a cheaply bound photocopy of *Le Roi en Jaune* I had found in a bookseller's stall in Paris in the mid-1980s[1]. Private readings were held in 1996 and 1997, and the last of these was attended by members of a local theatrical company, who expressed interest in performing the translation on stage.

For possibly the first time since its publication, on the weekend of Walpurgisnacht 1999, four showings of *The King in Yellow* were performed at the old Capital Theater in Olympia, Washington. The dead author's curse was not limited to the phantoms conjured by the script: there were theatre and personnel problems of all descriptions. Even the technical staff insisted that ghosts were disrupting their work; on opening night, just hours before curtain, the theatre's lights inexplicably failed and were only repaired literally as the show was starting.

The format of this, the first English edition in over a century, replicates as nearly as possible the original French edition of 1890. I salute the courage of the publishers, who feel as I do that this work, so radical and insinuating for its time, deserves at last to be reprinted.

Tacoma, Washington
9 September, 1999

---

1. To my knowledge, this was the only known copy of the original work. Sadly, it perished in a fire shortly after I completed this translation.

Acknowledgements

I WOULD LIKE TO THANK the many people who helped bring *The King in Yellow* to an unprepared and unsuspecting public, including especially the cast and crew of the 1999 production. My deepest gratitude to:

Corey Snow, for producing the 1999 show: a quixotic and financially ruinous undertaking that he nevertheless embraced with infectious enthusiasm, unrepentant dedication, and some seriously reckless driving.

Melanie Guknes, for daring to give form to my crazed vision. She made possible everything that followed.

Beverly Ryng, without whom I might have gone mad that much sooner.

John Tynes, who understood. Tell me, brother, have you found it?

Finally, I am indebted to *Scott Glancy*, who against his better judgement did not shoot his way out of the theatre during the press rehearsal.

Thank you all.

Thom Ryng

Cast of the 1999 Production

Alar:	Tara Lee Walling
Aldones:	Nathan Helsabeck
Bicree:	Thom Ryng
Bremchas:	Jake Newfield
Camilla:	Yulya Deych
Cassilda:	Samantha Chandler
Guard One / Guest:	Sarah McCracken
Guard Two / Guest:	Robin Scrivano
Guard / Guest:	Christopher Scrivano
Naotalba:	Forest Fousel
Stranger:	Corey Snow
Thale:	Amanda Lawn
Uoht / Guest:	Ron Monson
Brotherhood of the Yellow Sign:	as themselves
Director:	Melanie Guknes
Producer:	Corey Snow
Stage Manager:	Chelsie Davis
Art Director:	Steve Cagg
Technical Director:	Laura Conn

Performed at the historic Capitol Theater
in Olympia, Washington on Walpurgisnacht
April 30 through May 2, 1999.

Dramatis Personæ:

Alar: .... The Captain of the Guard
Aldones: .... A Prince, the brother of Cassilda
Bicree: .... A Guard of the Watch
Bremchas: .... A Guard of the Watch
Camilla: .... A Princess, the daughter of Cassilda
Cassilda: .... The Queen of Yhtill
Naotalba: .... The High Priest of Yhtill
King: .... An unnameable God
Stranger: .... The Phantom of Truth: a Messenger
Thale: .... A Prince, the older son of Cassilda
Uoht: .... A Prince, the younger son of Cassilda

Brotherhood of the Yellow Sign
Festival Guests
Guards of the Watch

Scene:
In the city of Yhtill, on the world of Hastur;
in and around the palace of the Queen.

Time:
Two days in the distant past or distant future.

THE
KING IN YELLOW

Prologue

Overture: "Irik Chuduk," a traditional Touvan lament.

A room in the palace of Yhtill. The room is sparsely furnished and threadbare. There is a balcony window to the left, overlooking a lake. The sky is pink and two red suns can be seen setting in the lake. There is an archway to the right. An old sword and a tapestry depicting a girl jumping over the horns of a bull hang upon the wall.

(Cassilda is at the window as the curtain rises. She is wearing a simple, elegant dress and a silver diadem.)

(The Stranger, who here serves as chorus, is dressed in black robes downstage at right. The Yellow Sign is embroidered on his robes, and his face is blank, featureless, and paper white.)

Stranger: Broods in her chambers Queen Cassilda;
Mourns she for her passing empty days.
Her dreams disturb the Lake of Hali
Where that ancient prophet's body lays.

In the constellation Hyades
Twin suns are setting in the waters.
Long grow shadows in the minds of men
As lengthen shadows on those waters.

Broods in her chambers Queen Cassilda,
Bearing full the weight of closing mists
And visions glimpsed of lost Carcosa
Throwing towers skyward from the depths.

Cassilda: The suns drown in the Lake of Hali as truth drowns in æons of accumulated wisdom. High Priest Naotalba shows me the ancient prophecies which say 'tis the Last King who reigns after me, and yet my brother Aldones pesters me to name an heir. The Hyades and Aldebaran are reflected in the lake, and there I see that dark and mythic city—I see Carcosa and the horrible truth of it drains my very breath. I know now that the end is coming. I'm dying. And already the scavengers circle.

Between Naotalba and Aldones I am in a vise. If I can just survive it, I shall have triumphed over both. But there, on the opposite shore... am I mad or dying?

(ENTER Camilla from right, carrying two dresses.)

Camilla: Do you like the blue one or the green one, mother?

Cassilda: (Distracted.) I'm dying.

Camilla: What are you going to wear tomorrow for the festival?

Cassilda: Every now and then, when I look across the lake at twilight, I imagine I see Carcosa on the far shore.

Camilla: Don't be ridiculous, mother. I'm trying to ask a serious question, and you're talking about cities that aren't there. If Carcosa were on the other side of the lake, don't you think that someone might have noticed it by now?

Cassilda: I'm sorry, dear. I've been reading some of the old stories lately, and they have my mind working in strange ways.

Camilla: (Brightly, holding up the dresses.) Blue or green?

Cassilda: (Distracted.) Green, dear.

Camilla: *(Makes a face.)* Well. It's obvious you need to get out of these rooms. Why don't you come to the dance tomorrow?

Cassilda: *(Turns to Camilla and sees her for the first time. She gestures to the dresses.)* Another late rendezvous?

Camilla: Oh, mother. It's nothing like that. Do you really like the green one better?

Cassilda: It's just fine dear. They're both lovely. Are you going out?

Camilla: Don't wait up.

Cassilda: I never do. Have you seen Uoht?

Camilla: Not since dinner. I think he went into the library.

(Cassilda turns back to the window. Camilla waits a moment, then shrugs her shoulders and EXITS to right.)

Cassilda: *(Softly.)* But I *do* see it.

(CURTAIN)

Act I, Scene I

A Courtyard in the Palace of Yhtill, overlooking the Lake of Hali. The sky is dark, dusky rose and there are many stars. Upstage is a colonnade of pillars and arches, and a few small potted trees. There is a stone bench downstage to the left. The scene begins in the evening and continues until the morning.

(ENTER Bicree from right and Bremchas from left. Bremchas is tall and wears a heavy beard; Bicree is short, thickset, and clean-shaven. They are both dressed in grey uniforms, similar to those of the Cossacks, and they are armed with muskets. Bremchas leans heavily upon his.)

Bicree: Hail, Bremchas, how went your watch?

Bremchas: My pants are wet and I have no money.

Bicree: By that you mean that all goes well?

Bremchas: The towers of Carcosa are behind the rising moon.

Bicree: Bremchas, you idiot, have you been drinking on your watch again? You're grinning like a madman.

Bremchas: Oh, friend Bicree, have you not seen the Yellow Sign? Have you not tasted of the pomegranate which whistles in the dark of the night through the teeth of a thousand dancing angels? *(He sobs.)* Have you not *seen* the stars turn one by one to black?

Bicree: So you have been drinking, and heavily, too, I'll warrant. It's a wonder the Captain hasn't beat some sense into you yet. Well, be off with you then; I relieve you of your duty.

Bremchas: *(Brightly.)* Oh, aye then.

(Bremchas salutes and staggeringly EXITS right, spinning once or twice around his musket.)

Bicree: *(Muttering.)* I don't know what to do with him. Every night is worse than the last. *(Louder.)* What sound is that? Who approaches?

(ENTER Aldones from right, hooded.)

Aldones: Only I, guardsman, the prince.

Bicree: Aye, one of many. No doubt your cloak hides your sword. Come closer that I might see your face.

(Aldones approaches and lowers his hood.)

Aldones: It is I, prince Aldones, brother of the Queen.

Bicree: *(Kneels.)* My lord, I had no idea... it's so late...

Aldones: Rise, good guard. A prince keeps such hours as he may. Yes rise, and look at me. I am not some terrible god of the gibbering priests, but a man. *(Bicree stands.)* Much better. Tell me, good guard, who was that man I just passed?

Bicree: Oh, my lord, that was Bremchas, my comrade, a guardsmen like myself, but off duty...

Aldones: Has the man been drinking?

Bicree: Well, my lord, Bremchas is off duty now, and to be honest even when he hasn't tipped the bottle, he's a bit tipped, if you take my meaning, my lord.

Aldones: Yes, I understand. Perhaps you would like some time to look after your comrade?

Bicree: Oh, my lord, I've just come on duty and won't be relieved until four bells. Besides, good old Bremchas can look after himself, and his lackey can mop up the spewlings (begging your lordship's pardon) the, ah, vomit, my lord.

Aldones: Have you been in the guard long, Corporal... ah...

Bicree: Bicree, my lord, my name's Bicree. I'm on the guards near six months now, my lord.

Aldones: Then good Bicree, I forgive your fault. If a prince of the blood tells you to leave your post, then you must have no fear that you are deserting your duty. I shall tell Captain Alar that I have relieved you for the hour.

Bicree: Why, thank you, my lord! *(Turns around, thinks better of it, then turns back.)* Do you need a musket?

Aldones: No good guard, I have my sword under my cloak, remember?

Bicree: Of course my lord, how stupid of me. Thank you, my lord, a hundred thanks, the gods keep you...

Aldones: *(Aside.)* Not if I can help it.

Bicree: ...Good night, my lord. In an hour, then.

Aldones: An hour.

(Bicree EXITS right, bowing repeatedly.)

Aldones: Jabbering ape, will they let anyone into the guards these days? Two have I seen this night, one drunk and the other a simpleton. My father would never have allowed it, and yet my dear sister Cassilda chooses guardsmen on the basis of whosoever shall fit into one of the old uniforms. Dances and balls and masquerades she attends instead of drills and marches. Evermore our empire constricts about us as a noose about a common thief. Every day one of our governors suffers some new indignity at the hands of the mob, and no week goes by without news of some town or another sacked by the rabble. No soldiers can be dispatched, no new armies raised, but our ladies somehow have the most sumptuous finery to be found on three continents.

But while the Queen, my sister, and her prancing court dance in their maddening and ever contracting circles, I at least have laid plans for the future: I mean to wear Cassilda's crown and reconquer our lost heritage. I should have been king; I'm the older. But a weakness of my father for the girl—his only weakness it was—has proved our undoing. I shall allow that spurn to spur me to greatness and into the throne which should have been mine. I shall use whatever means present themselves, for I offer to Yhtill a future—not an eternal present. I will establish a new order and save our empire from degradation and decline.

Had I been king, High Priest Naotalba and his chanting clique of charlatans would have been arrested and their irrational revolutionary incantations suppressed. We must have rationality. Had I been king, I would not have allowed the structure of the court and of the army to come unraveled as Cassilda did. We must have structure. Had I been king, the first rioters at Sparos would have been slaughtered, and the civil order maintained. We must have order!

And now, my moment has come: the Queen my sister thinks that she is dying, and yet somehow remains so blind to the future that she has not even chosen an heir, probably for fear the paperwork might interfere with her dancing. And which of her children could she choose anyway? Camilla is ruled by her emotions; she would never do. Thale would be even worse; the boy has a quick mind, but he's owned by the priests. And then there's Uoht who does anything... But wait, someone approaches. *(Draws up hood.)*

(ENTER Uoht from right, hooded.)

Aldones: Who approaches?

Uoht: I was not aware that guardsmen held their posts unarmed.

Aldones: I have a sword under my cloak. I say again, who's there?

Uoht: *(Loudly.)* You dare...! Know you not that only a noble may bear a blade, even in jest? And you an unwashed soldier! What right have you? *(Approaches and draws sword.)* Answer quick or I'll cut you down you, you scoundrel! *(Waves sword ineffectually at Aldones.)* Fall to your knees and beg my forgiveness!

Aldones: *(Drops hood.)* Is all of Yhtill populated by morons?

Uoht: Uncle!

Aldones: Is this how you approach a secret meeting, Uoht? With shouts and curses? I'm frankly amazed that you didn't alert the entire watch with that show. The whole point of meeting in this obscure courtyard was to avoid attention, not to draw it.

Uoht: I'm sorry, uncle, but surely no prince of the blood could allow a mere guard to challenge them? And so rudely? You must see my point.

Aldones: The only point I see is that silly sword. Put it away before you hurt yourself.

Uoht: Yes, uncle. *(Sheathes sword.)*

Aldones: Now, have you brought it?

Uoht: The seal? I have it here. Should mother find it missing...

Aldones: The Queen can't find it most days when it's there, much less when it's not. Let us go to the bench and do the thing.

(Aldones and Uoht retire to the bench, stage left. Aldones slowly puts his hand into his cloak. He hesitates a moment, then pulls out a thick scroll of papers. He unrolls them and places them on the bench. Uoht moves to his side.)

(ENTER Thale and Naotalba from right.)

(During the next exchange between Thale and Naotalba, Aldones holds out his hand and Uoht quickly pulls a seal from his cloak and hands it to him. Aldones hands a pen to Uoht. Uoht kneels before the bench and begins to write on various of the pages before him. Aldones fondles the seal, turning it over and over in his hands, occasionally looking up into the distance. Uoht elbows Aldones in the leg; Aldones does not notice. Uoht elbows him again, more insistently, and Aldones looks down, startled. Aldones applies wax and seal to several of the papers. He should do this just prior to speaking his next line.)

(This entire transaction should be strictly mundane and should form an unobtrusive background to the following dialogue.)

Thale: But reverend father, many things in the teachings still trouble my thoughts.

Naotalba: What is it that troubles you, my prince?

Thale: Firstly, reverend father, if the god of our world is so terrible that he cannot be named, how knows he that our supplications and prayers are to him?

Naotalba: My prince, there are mysteries the answers to which man has not the wisdom to attend.

Thale: But that reply may serve any question. Why does the Avatar of our god dress in tattered rags and a yellow veil?

Naotalba: The King in Yellow may dress how he pleases, but the ancients said that his every rag serves to hide our city from its enemies. Is it not written "The scalloped tatters of the King in Yellow must hide Yhtill forever?"

Thale: Very well, reverend father. Why then must we seek the Yellow Sign?

Naotalba: So many questions, my prince! The Yellow Sign is the announcement, the calling card if you will, of the King in Yellow. If the King's dead city of Carcosa manifests itself, then the sign is inevitable. If the Yellow Sign can be found, the transcendence will be at hand and the King in Yellow will lead us into a new age, a new... wait. *(Grabs Thale's arm.)* Is that not your uncle, there?

Thale: Aye, reverend father, and my brother too. They look busy. I'm sure they don't wish to be bothered. I mean, why else would they be about this time of night in this court so distant from their palace rooms? Let us retreat from here...

Naotalba: Courage, my prince! You cannot always flee. Perhaps instead it is time to test your skills. Remember you the "Unseeing Eye?"

Thale: Aye, the invisibility chant. I know it.

Naotalba: Then chant it with me now, that we may learn what mischief your brother and uncle are about.

(Naotalba and Thale chant, as follows. Their voices should fade near the end, during which time a spot of violet light envelops them, to remain until the end of the scene.)

(Chant): Oodás horasa mae,
gar esómí aorotos
hós exaphistamí Karkósas
Tráchuí homichálí
kruptá mae,
kí hostis an dé-erchontí
esontí tuphlon.

(Naotalba and Thale move closer to Aldones and Uoht.)

Aldones: There, the thing is done.

(Uoht scrambles to his feet.)

Uoht: *(Doubtfully.)* It is for the good of the city that we do this thing...

Aldones: Of course, nephew, of course. Your mother is too busy to arrange the succession herself; it is a kindness we do, to arrange it for her. You are now your mother's heir.

Uoht: But I am too young to be king.

Aldones: Then it is fortunate that your mother yet lives.

Uoht: But what about Thale?

Aldones: Thale is a slate, a rudderless schooner at the mercy of the wind. He is unfit to be king. *(Hands seal back to Uoht, who places it inside his cloak.)* Go and take the seal back to its chamber. I shall keep the papers until I can deposit them in the archives tomorrow. The guard will return presently, and even he might become uneasy if he found you here with me. Off with you.

Uoht: Yes uncle. Until tomorrow, then?

Aldones: Off with you.

(Uoht EXITS to right.)

Aldones: A near thing. My next appointment is at half past the hour, and the time is nearly at hand. The plan unfolds, and soon that nitwit child and his sister will be the first removed.

(ENTER Bremchas staggering from right; he has lost his musket.)

Bremchas: *(To Thale and Naotalba.)* Good morrow, misty fellows!

Thale: *(Frantically.)* He sees us!

Naotalba: *(Motions Thale to remain still.)* He cannot, my prince, he hails the moons setting behind us. Quiet now!

Aldones: You there, be off with you. Go home.

Bremchas: But surely, my lord, you have seen Carcosa with its towers rising behind the moons? We have no homes now to call our own.

THE KING IN YELLOW

Aldones: Be off with you, drunkard, before I call the watch upon you.

Bremchas: The fool's upon you, my noble friend, for I am the watch. It's you that should be off... off... off sailing a mastless schooner upon the dark and glassy waters of Lake Hali, to where Carcosa currently reclines.

Aldones: Carcosa is a myth, you idiot, and there's no city upon the lake except Yhtill. You're hallucinating. Go home and sleep it off.

Bremchas: *(Sings idiotically and capers about.)*
I'm dancing in a flesh garden
with vine and weed and flower,
The last is lost, the second dead,
the first seeks out his power!
I'm dancing where the flames will strike,
and comes an unknown king,
To give us what we think we need,
taking everything!
(Bows to Thale and Naotalba.)
Good evening, my lords, I hope you get your sight back.
(Shouts to Aldones.) Good night, false guard!

(ENTER Camilla from right. She wears the blue dress with a hooded cape.)

Bremchas: *(To Camilla.)* Fare thee well, foolish unmasker!

(EXIT Bremchas to right, capering grotesquely.)

Camilla: *(Removes hood.)* What a strange man.

Thale: *(Whispers.)* My sister Camilla!

Camilla: Uncle Aldones? Is that you?

Aldones: Ah, Camilla! Thank you for agreeing to see me.

Camilla: *(Moves past Thale and Naotalba to bench; she sits.)* Now what is it that you needed to see me about, so late and so far from a decent fire?

Aldones: I decided secrecy was best. You weren't followed?

Camilla: No. Nobody saw me leave. Who was that strange little man?

Aldones: A drunkard of the guards, I think.

Camilla: He's not drunk; he's mad.

Aldones: You can see just how far the guards have declined since your grandfather died. In his day, drunkards like him visited the Torturer's chambers.

Camilla: What is it you wished to tell me? I feel very cold out here.

Aldones: It's not that cold; the Hyades are warm and close tonight.

Camilla: I feel some chill in the wind, and I shiver.

Aldones: I know your time is precious, so I'll come to the point of it. Your brother Uoht has stolen the great seal and has forged papers saying that your mother has named him as her heir.

Camilla: *(Shocked, she stands.)* No!

Aldones: It's true, I'm afraid.

Camilla: But he's still just a boy. He loves mother. How could he do that? Why would he... surely you don't feel... ?

Aldones: I don't know what to think. I cannot believe that he means your mother harm...

Camilla: Not Uoht!

Aldones: I have the papers here. *(Pulls the scroll from his cloak and unrolls it.)* He told me to file them with the chancellery in the morning. Is this not his handwriting? Is this not his mark?

Camilla: *(Steps back.)* What are you going to do with them? Have you told mother?

Aldones: *(Rolls scroll and places it back in his robe.)* How could I tell the Queen that her favourite son was conspiring against her? I asked you here because you're closer to the Queen than I. You must tell her. If I don't deposit these in the archives, Uoht will become suspicious. And if he's capable of conspiring against his own mother...

Camilla: I can't believe it.

Aldones: You have seen the proof of it yourself.

Camilla: What should we do?

Aldones: Perhaps you should tell your mother that Uoht has stolen the seal...

Camilla: She'd never believe it. *(Frowns, then brightens.)* Unless she saw the papers.

Aldones: They'll be on file tomorrow. Of course, by that time who knows what he will have done.

Camilla: Oh! He wouldn't... wouldn't *kill* mother, would he? Oh, what shall we do?

Aldones: I suppose you could have him detained.

Camilla: No. Yes! Maybe we could have the guard detain him in the Dhooric Tower?

Aldones: A most excellent idea.

Camilla: Yes. Yes, I'll do it.

Aldones: What do you want me to do to aid this plan of yours?

Camilla: *(Frowns.)* Well... don't tell anybody. The fewer people who know about this the better.

Aldones: *(Prompting.)* So, the guard will arrest the Prince in the palace...

Camilla: Oh no! That would never do, would it? Maybe we could ask him to meet us here? And then arrest him?

Aldones: A capital plan, my dear. You will make a fine Queen some day.

Camilla: *(Distracted.)* Yes, I'll send him a message to meet me here on urgent business, and the guard will be here to arrest him. *(Louder, to Aldones.)* Thank you, uncle; I have ever so much to do.

Aldones: You had best get started.

Camilla: Yes, uncle. Good night.

Aldones: Good night.

Camilla: Shall I see you at the dance tomorrow night?

Aldones: *(Forcing a smile.)* Oh, I couldn't miss it, could I?

Camilla: *(Oblivious.)* No, of course not. Good night again.

(EXIT Camilla to right. At this point, Naotalba is staring off into the distance of the Lake. The arches of the colonnade are beginning to melt, but this is not what he is looking at.)

Aldones: There's the second part of my plan in place. Camilla will cause her brother's arrest, and once he is in the tower, it will be a small matter to kill him, leaving Camilla the blame. A good night's work, this. And here is the guard, as scheduled. *(Shouts, to right.)* Who approaches?

(ENTER Bicree from right. He walks between Thale and Naotalba.)

Bicree: Your relief, my lord.

Aldones: And how fares bumpkin?

Bicree: Bremchas, my lord? I couldn't find him in the barracks, so I slipped off to see my girl. *(Hastily.)* I didn't see no harm in it.

Aldones: No, that's fine. You're a good man... ah...

Bicree: *(Prompting.)* Bicree.

Aldones: Of course, Bicree. You're a good man, Bicree. I shall leave you to your duty.

Bicree: Very good. And thank you, my lord.

(EXIT Aldones to right. He does not look back.)

(Bicree looks after him for a moment. During the next exchange between Thale and Naotalba, Bicree sits down on the bench. He takes a thin yellow book from his pocket and begins to read it. It is titled The King in Yellow.)

Thale: Reverend father, what shall we do?

Naotalba: *(Softly.)* Carcosa!

Thale: I beg your pardon?

Naotalba: Tell me, boy, what do you see over there?

Thale: Again? *(Sighs, then clasps hands behind back and recites.)* "What view my child, from the palace? What view my child from the temple gate?..."

Naotalba: But what do you see?

Thale: *(Continues.)* "I see the Hyades reflecting in the calm, black waters of the Lake of Hali...."

Naotalba: *(Prompting.)* And?

Thale: *(Continues reciting.)* "I see the cloudy depths of Demhe, the greater moon."

Naotalba: *(Desperate.)* Nothing else?

Thale: Have I not repeated the litany as the fathers instructed? Do you expect me to see Carcosa as well?

Naotalba: *(Small.)* Do you not?

Thale: Reverend father, are you quite all right? I think perhaps we should go inside. It is uncommonly cold this night, and at your age...

Naotalba: *(Hisses.)* Look again!

Thale: *(Humouring Naotalba, he recites.)* "What view my child, from the palace? What view my child from the temple gate? I see the Hyades reflecting in the calm, black waters of the Lake of Hali. I see the

	cloudy depths of Demhe, the greater moon. And..." *(Confusion.)* and...
Naotalba:	And?
Thale:	*(Clasps Naotalba's arm to steady himself.)* Dear gods. Dear gods, I... I see it. It's true.
Naotalba:	Surely the time of transcendence is at hand!
Thale:	*(Distant.)* What now?
Naotalba:	What now? We must seek the Yellow Sign! Come, boy! We must consult the runes!
Thale:	But what of my uncle? His plots and...
Naotalba:	The world is a place more subtle and irrational than your uncle realizes. Let him plot, it will avail him nothing. The power of the government is ending. All human power is ending, and we shall rule Hastur now! What matters your uncle's plans? What matters your mother's will?
Thale:	But my brother Uoht will be here—the guard will arrest him. Surely we can wait a few moments to warn him?
Naotalba:	*(Firmly.)* Irrelevant. When we rule this world, what matters the petty politics of this city?
Thale:	But we don't rule yet. Yhtill is our home. And Uoht my brother...
Naotalba:	Then you can see that there is no time to waste! To the temple, boy! We can release your brother when *we* are in command. We can send Aldones to the tower in his stead if you wish. But right now, time is everything. Unless we find the Yellow Sign,

	Carcosa may fade from view again, and then all will be lost!
Thale:	But...
Naotalba:	*(Pushing Thale to right.)* To the temple!
Thale:	But...

(EXIT Thale and Naotalba to right as a troop of guards led by Alar ENTER past them. Captain Alar is a woman in her thirties with a severe haircut. Her uniform is black and covered with gold, but otherwise similar to that of the guards.)

Alar:	*(Shouting.)* Corporal Bicree!
Bicree:	*(Jumps up from bench, losing his book in the process.)* Captain Alar!
Alar:	At ease, Corporal. I'll send Private Bremchas to relieve you shortly.
Bicree:	Bremchas, Captain? But I just relieved Bremchas this past watch, Captain, and he's not quite right...
Alar:	Dammit Bicree, can't be helped. Most of the guard has been dispatched into the city for the festival. The rest of us are here on this damnedable mission to arrest some damnfool prince or another.
Bicree:	*(Surprised.)* A prince, Captain?
Alar:	Damn right, Bicree. But you don't know a thing about it, understand? Orders from above and all that.
Bicree:	*(Confused.)* Yes, Captain. I mean, no, Captain.

Alar: Damn good show, Bicree. You'll make sergeant yet; I love you like a damned son.

Bicree: Thank you, Captain.

Alar: Now, cover your eyes.

Bicree: Captain?

Alar: Cover your eyes Corporal. With your hands.

Bicree: Cover my eyes, Captain?

Alar: Dammit Corporal, am I speaking in Urdu? Cover your damn eyes. And turn around while you're at it.

Bicree: *(Doubtfully.)* Yes, Captain. *(He turns around and covers his eyes.)*

Alar: The fewer who know about this damned operation, the happier the Princess. The happier the Princess, the sooner we can all get back to bed. *(Addressing the guard.)* You lot there—hide. Lay an ambuscade.

(Members of the guard look about helplessly. Eventually, they all hide in totally ineffectual places. One crouches behind a potted plant, one hides under the bench, etc. One even hides behind Bicree.)

Alar: Damn good show, damn good show.

(A short time passes. The guards fidget. The guard under the bench picks up Bicree's book and begins to read. Several of the guards yawn.)

Alar: Dammit all, I thought punctuality was the politeness of princes, or some such rot. Where is that boy?

(Another short wait.)

Alar: Dammit all, where—ah! *(Shouts to right.)* Who approaches, there?

Uoht: *(Offstage to right.)* Camilla?

Alar: What kind of a damned name for a boy is "Camilla?"

(ENTER Uoht from right. His sword is out.)

Uoht: What did you say?

Alar: Dammit, boy, I don't even *know* Urdu, and if your name's Camilla then I'm Prince Thale. Answer the damned question: who approaches?

Uoht: I am prince Uoht, guard, and I don't take kindly to your tone. If I weren't here to meet my sister Camilla, I'd run you through where you stand.

Alar: Oh you *would*, would you? Damned rapscallion. And here I was afraid I wouldn't enjoy this.

Uoht: What? Do you know who you're talking to? *(Drawing himself up.)* I am a prince of the blood, and you shall pay most dearly for that insult. Defend yourself, peasant.

(Uoht attacks Alar with his sword and they fight for a few moments, Alar using her musket as a polearm. Alar is easily repelling Uoht's furious attacks. The guards reveal themselves and slowly advance on the pair.)

Uoht: What is the meaning of this? Help, I'm ambushed! It's a revolution! Help!

(One of the guard brings the butt of his musket down on Uoht's head, rendering the prince unconscious.)

Alar: Damned impertinent. You lot there—take him to the Dhooric Tower and lock him up. Put him in the cell with the cutpurse.

(Guard pick up Uoht and his sword and EXIT right, carrying them.)

Alar: You, there. Corporal Bicree!

Bicree: Yes, Captain?

Alar: As you were, Bicree. I'll send Bremchas to relieve you.

Bicree: Very good, Captain. *(He turns around and salutes.)*

Alar: Good night, Corporal. *(She returns the salute.)* Damned good show.

Bicree: Yes, Captain. Thank you, Captain.

(EXIT Alar right. Bicree turns around to face left. The melting of the arches accelerates as reality begins to come undone. Offstage to left is heard the soft, distant sound of a gong. Suddenly surprised, Bicree readies his musket.)

Bicree: Who approaches?

Stranger: *(Offstage to left, a grating, inhuman voice.)* Weary travelers, to a new home come we.

Bicree: Say, where are you from, anyway? How did you get past the city watch at this time of night?

Stranger: From the city of a great king come I.

Bicree: Come closer that I might see you. The rest of you stay back.

(ENTER Stranger from left. He wears a hooded white cloak, with the Yellow Sign embroidered on a black circle on both sleeves. His voice is insistent and grating, almost buzzing, like the sound of insects in the night. He has great difficulty speaking.)

Stranger: Here am I.

(ENTER Camilla, Cassilda, two guards, and Bremchas from right. The guards should be straightening their uniforms, putting on hats, etc., as if they were just woken up. Bremchas has his musket back and a wide grin on his face.)

Cassilda: *(Angry.)* What is the meaning of this torch lit parade into the gardens of my palace?

Bicree: *(Turns.)* Your majesty!

Cassilda: *(Coldly.)* Explain, guard, and to my satisfaction, how fifty torches could have formed a parade to the palace and not be stopped? Why was no alarm raised? If I hadn't seen them from my window, I would still not know they were here. Well? Answer! Or does your tongue function only slightly less well than your eyes?

Bicree: But your majesty...

Cassilda: *(Interrupting.)* Yes?

Bicree: Well, I... I didn't see them.

Cassilda: *(Increasingly louder.)* You didn't see them? You didn't see them? You didn't *see* them? *(Turns to Guard One.)* Guard, take this man to the infirmary and ask the surgeon to determine whether he suffers from exhaustion or blindness.

Guard One: Yes, my Queen. *(Salutes.)*

(EXIT Guard One and Bicree to right. Bicree drags his musket behind him.)

Cassilda: *(Turning to Stranger.)* Now, who are you?

Stranger: Truth am I. From the city of a great king to a new home come I.

(The Stranger throws back his hood, revealing the Pallid Mask, a face blank of features and paper white.)

Camilla: Look at him!

Cassilda: *(Softly.)* Listen to him.

Stranger: The Pallid Mask is it. Be worn by my Brotherhood must it.

Cassilda: *(Uncertainly.)* So you are an ambassador?

Stranger: Truth am I. From the city of a great king to a new home come I.

Cassilda: 'Tis passing strange that we weren't expecting you.

Camilla: But you know how bad the roads are now, mother. Maybe the message didn't arrive?

Stranger: Many messages has sent my king.

Cassilda: We must apologize that there were none to meet you at the gates.

Stranger: Misunderstand the messages perhaps did ye?

Cassilda: This distinguished member of our royal guard will escort you and your party to suitable rooms. You

	will be presented at Court during the festival tomorrow, and I shall receive you there.
Stranger:	Objections none have we. Rest need we.
Cassilda:	*(To Guard Two.)* Take the ambassador and his party to the Summer Wing. I don't care who you have to wake up, but make sure that our guests here are comfortable.
Guard Two:	Yes, my Queen. *(Salutes.)*

(EXIT Guard Two and Stranger to right. The Brotherhood files onstage from left, and offstage to right. They are dressed in white hooded robes and each carries two torches, one in each hand. The last one has a small gong which he chimes every three steps or so.)

(By this time, the melted pillars and arches of the colonnade look decidedly organic, as though the courtyard were inside the rib cage of some gigantic, buried beast.)

Camilla:	*(Brightly.)* Mother, I've just had the most marvelous idea!
Cassilda:	*(Exhausted.)* Have you?
Camilla:	Yes! Let's turn the dance tomorrow into a costume ball! We could have everyone wear those Pallid Masks, and nobody would know who anybody else was! Wouldn't that be just delicious?
Cassilda:	And I thought that you were the rational one in the family.
Camilla:	Please mother?
Cassilda:	Camilla, 'tis nearly morning. I'm sure this won't seem like such a good idea after a few hours of sleep.

Camilla:	Please mother? It'll be such fun not knowing who's who, don't you think?
Cassilda:	Camilla...
Camilla:	Please?
Cassilda:	Oh, very well. But you'll have to arrange it...
Camilla:	Oh, I will!
Cassilda:	...in the morning.
Camilla:	Oh, thank you, mother! Thank you! Good night! *(Kisses Cassilda on the cheek and turns to leave.)*
Cassilda:	Now, what was it that you came in to tell me before all this excitement started?
Camilla:	*(Turns back briefly before continuing.)* Oh, I don't remember. I'm sure it was nothing.

(EXIT Camilla to right.)

Cassilda:	Good night, then, Camilla. *(Turns to Bremchas.)* Can you stand a better watch than your comrade did?
Bremchas:	Of course, my queen, for I can see, Where blind was my friend Corporal Bicree! *(Laughs slightly.)*
Cassilda:	*(Yawns.)* Good. Then you can take the rest of his watch. *(Turns to leave.)*
Bremchas:	Why, I even dread Carcosa see On the far banks of the Lake of Hali!
Cassilda:	*(Turns back, sharply.)* What? What did you say?

Bremchas: *(Firmly, as if reciting.)*
Carcosa throws her towers to the sky
Above the Lake of Hali, and the moons
Set silently before them in the night.
(Points to lake.) Look!

Cassilda: I do see it! I do. What does this mean that others see it as well? Can it still be a delusion?

Bremchas: It's no delusion if two share it, your majesty. It's real.

Cassilda: Then all is lost! But wait, I haven't found the Yellow Sign.

Bremchas: *(Seriously.)* Perhaps there is time yet to save us?

Cassilda: The Yellow Sign must not be found. I must speak to my son Thale and see what he learns from the priest.

Bremchas: *(Grinning again.)* Indeed?

Cassilda: Perhaps he can at last be of some use.

Bremchas: Everybody should be useful, don't you think?

Cassilda: *(Moves to left, muttering.)* Yes, perhaps Thale will know something. Between Naotalba and Aldones I am in a vise.

(EXIT Cassilda to left.)

Bremchas: *(Calling after Cassilda.)* Good night, fair Queen! And good day to night, for here rise the twin suns!

(CURTAIN)

Act I, Scene II

Music: "Mandukhai" an old Mongolian air.

A great hall in the Palace of Yhtill. Upstage center is a large stone throne, unoccupied, with a wooden paneled curving behind it, depicting writhing dragons. Flanking the throne are tapestries bearing the image of the Hyades. A table with food and drinks is downstage from the throne. There is a large balcony to the left, overlooking the courtyard and the lake.

The large, multi-towered city of Carcosa is quite obviously visible on the far bank, and several of the towers are tall enough to reach out of sight into the sky. The sky outside is pink and there are many stars and a small misshapen moon which, as it sets, moves in front of the towers of Carcosa. The right entrance is composed of three arches. The entire room is festively decorated. A masked ball is being held and a swirling party atmosphere predominates. From time to time small bits of plaster and dust fall from the ceiling into the drinks and food of the guests, who pick them out and continue their conversations, heedless.

During the course of the scene, the stars outside the balcony change one by one to black. By the time of the Stranger's entrance, they are all darkened like holes in the sky.

(Cassilda, Camilla, Aldones, Alar, and guests are dressed in their finery and in Pallid Masks. Thale and Naotalba are in their robes, also with Pallid Masks. These masks should consist of a blank, face-shaped sheet of thin wood or cardboard which the various players and guests hold to their face by means of a short stick. The guests are chatting animatedly amongst themselves, some briefly removing their masks as they do so. A band plays quietly.)

(Cassilda pulls away from the crowd to stand before the throne. The room quiets and the band stops playing.)

Cassilda: *(Sings.)*
Along the shore the cloud waves break,
The twin suns sink behind the lake,
The shadows lengthen
          In Carcosa.

Strange is the night where black stars rise,
And strange moons circle through the skies,
But stranger still is
          Lost Carcosa.

Songs that the Hyades shall sing,
Where flap the tatters of the King,
Must die unheard in
          Dim Carcosa.

Song of my soul, my voice is dead,
Die thou, unsung, as tears unshed
Shall dry and die in
          Lost Carcosa.

(Polite, but scattered applause from the gathering crowd.)

Naotalba: *(Aside to Thale.)* She sings of Carcosa! How much does she know? Could it be she who thought for us to wear the prophesied Pallid Mask?

Thale: However much she knows, reverend father, her fears are far greater. She thinks that she is dying, rather, she thinks that we are killing her. She has not seen Carcosa.

Naotalba: Go to her. Find out from her whether or not she has seen it.

Thale: I doubt that she will talk to me.

Naotalba: You must try.

Thale: Very well, reverend father.

(Prodded by Naotalba, Thale approaches Cassilda who is walking downstage to the table.)

Thale: How are you mother?

Cassilda: Like my country, I'm old and dying.

Thale: *(Throws up hands in frustration.)* Does it have to be this way?

Cassilda: What do you mean?

Thale: It's no secret that you think I'm a disappointment.

Cassilda: Oh, Thale, you're my son. So long as you're happy, you can't really disappoint me.

Thale: You've never approved of my decision to enter the priesthood.

Cassilda: Well, how could I? The priesthood shall be the death of the empire.

Thale: You're obsessed with death. That prophecy was made a long time ago, when the first king Thale drowned Hali in the lake and the Yellow Sign was lost.

Cassilda: 'Tis nothing to do with any prophecy. The priesthood is draining the blood of the empire, waxing powerful in our waning days. And now their talons are sunk deep into our dynasty.

Thale: That's because the priesthood can offer something our dynasty no longer can—a future.

Cassilda: But the future they offer—*you* offer—is submission to a tatterdemalion demon of destruction.

Thale: Better destruction than decay.

Cassilda: But don't you see? 'Tis *our* destruction they preach—*you* preach. You are exchanging obedience to the Queen of Yhtill for obedience to the King in Yellow. You are turning away from action and thought, and surrendering to preordained fate. No, not fate—doom. Can't you see that the priesthood is feeding upon the empire as if 'twas carrion?

Thale: Mother, you're getting a little melodramatic.

Cassilda: Better melodramatic than mindless.

Thale: I'm sorry you feel that way.

(Thale turns and walks back to Naotalba as Camilla taps Cassilda on the shoulder. Cassilda turns to her.)

Camilla: Isn't this wonderful?

Cassilda: I... I needed to ask Thale about...

Camilla: You can ask him later. After that dreadful old song, I think that you need to dance.

Cassilda: *(Annoyed.)* Really, Camilla!

(Cassilda allows herself to be led upstage by Camilla. A great formal dance ensues, in which Cassilda, Camilla and many guests take part. Aldones, Thale, and Naotalba do not. Thale rejoins Naotalba at the balcony.)

Music: A waltz, slow and melancholy.

Naotalba: Well? Does she see it?

Thale: I... I don't know. We were talking past each other.

Naotalba: *(Suddenly angry.)* Idiot boy. Must I do everything?

Thale: Reverend father, if you have no use for me, I can certainly leave. There's no reason to get angry with me.

Naotalba: *(Starts as if to say something, then stops. He seems to physically shrink, and he rubs his tired eyes.)* I apologize, my prince. But this day has been a great strain upon me.

Thale: That's all right, reverend father.

Naotalba: Perhaps we should pursue other means of obtaining our answer. I shall speak with your uncle. He is the only member of your mother's court with any vision, no matter how self-serving.

Thale: If we must. I see him at the throne.

(Thale beckons to Aldones, who presently joins them.)

Aldones: Nephew! Are you still bewitched by this old faker?

Thale: *(Bows slightly.)* Uncle Aldones.

Aldones: Why stay with Naotalba? You're a prince of the blood. You don't need words for you may bear a sword...

Thale: They are much the same.

Aldones: ...or did you put that behind you as well when you abandoned our dynasty?

Thale: I did not abandon you; I moved beyond you.

Aldones: *(Laughs.)* To what, boy? Ragged gods, empty promises, or simple irrelevance?

Thale: *(Angering.)* Well, at least I haven't become a ruthless...

Naotalba: *(To Thale.)* Easy, boy.

Aldones: *(Suddenly suspicious.)* What do you mean by that?

Naotalba: The boy means nothing by it. He is... a little short tempered, that's all.

Aldones: Let Thale speak for himself.

Thale: I... we saw you in the courtyard last night.

Naotalba: Thale!

Thale: And we've seen Carcosa. Your wicked reign will end before it's even begun!

Aldones: *(Relaxing somewhat.)* Carcosa is a myth. The fact that Naotalba here has convinced you that you've seen it only proves my point: he has bewitched you. *(Mocking.)* It's all delusions—you're living in a fantasy world of dead prophets and living gods. You're worse than your mother.

Thale: I tell you I saw Carcosa. And I saw your plot against Uoht.

Naotalba: Carcosa is real.

Aldones: Yes, you've apparently convinced Queen Cassilda of that as well. Oh, don't look so surprised that the Queen shares your delusions. Both she and

	Camilla seem on the verge of some sort of breakdown. Imagine—taking the old prophesies as truth! And Camilla, well... these masks, you know, were her idea.
Naotalba:	*(Simultaneous, surprised.)* Camilla?
Thale:	*(Simultaneous, demanding.)* What about Uoht?
Aldones:	*(To Thale.)* What about him?
Thale:	You've had him jailed. You're after the throne.
Aldones:	*(Ever so sweetly.)* Why Thale, I'm surprised. If I had wanted the throne, why would I jail the only member of the dynasty too young to sit upon it? Do you imagine me that stupid?
Thale:	But Camilla...
Aldones:	Bah! The priest has addled your brains. And to think that I once favoured you as heir.
Naotalba:	It signifies nothing. Your father once favoured you as heir, Aldones, did he not?
Aldones:	*(Furious.)* My father was a sick old man when he changed the order of succession, a sick, addled old man. His will was broken by your droning idiocy.
Naotalba:	*(Nonplussed.)* Except for your father's final moment of clarity, your family has never shown the slightest evidence of will, only indolence punctured by the odd occasional panic.
Aldones:	A feeble insult, Naotalba, coming from a man who sees invisible cities. Your delusions shall be your end.

Naotalba: *(Sweetly.)* And your stubborn blindness shall be yours.

Aldones: We shall see.

(Aldones swirls about and melts into the crowd.)

Naotalba: I fear, my prince, that he is truly blind. I had hoped once that he, at least, of your dynasty could be persuaded to help us, to work for the creation of the new age, but he is more blind than the rest. Even the Queen has seen Carcosa where he has not.

Thale: *(Pondering.)* I wonder why that is...

Naotalba: Blindness, simple obstinate blindness. He is unwilling to see the truth, where it disagrees with his own version of it. Since we know the truth, we can more easily see it.

Thale: But reverend father, is it not possible that we see it because we are unwilling to accept the truth of its nonexistence? Or perhaps we misunderstand what we see? Or perhaps what we see is only a reflection of what's...

Naotalba: Thale, we are the sacred priesthood of the King in Yellow. How can we not correctly interpret the scriptures and the signs? Scripture reveals and signs foretell the coming days. We are living in the end times; who can deny it?

Thale: But what role will we play *after* the end? Are we so certain that we shall rule Yhtill when the King in Yellow returns?

Naotalba: The King in Yellow rules Carcosa, my prince, the city of the dying. We shall rule Yhtill, the city of the living.

Thale: *(Softly.)* But are we living, I wonder?

Naotalba: *(Chiding.)* Your speculations will lead you into nonsense if you are not careful, Brother Thale.

Thale: Yes, reverend father.

Naotalba: Now, let us proceed in our inquisition. Prince Aldones claims that the Queen has seen the city, and that Camilla has somehow seen the Pallid Mask. I think perhaps it is my turn to do some questioning—I will seek out Camilla while you stay here and out of trouble. Once we have a few answers, the search for the Yellow Sign can begin in earnest!

Thale: *(Sighs.)* Yes, reverend father.

(Thale and Naotalba melt into the crowd. Aldones approaches Alar, who is at the table piling food onto a plate.)

Aldones: Captain.

Alar: My lord.

Aldones: Brother Thale has accused me of plotting against my sister.

Alar: My lord?

Aldones: The priesthood must be stopped from spreading their lies.

Alar: Agreed, my lord.

Aldones: Arrest him.

Alar: Yes, my lord.

(Aldones melts into the crowd. Alar puts down her plate and moves to the balcony, where she meets with Thale.)

Alar: Greetings, priest.

Thale: *(Conversationally.)* Oh, I'm not a priest yet, just an acolyte. Do I know you?

Alar: Dammit, Thale. *(Pulls mask away.)*

Thale: Alar! I haven't seen you in, it must be...

Alar: Since you left for the damn seminary.

Thale: Three years?

Alar: Three damn years you've run away from me.

(A pause.)

Thale: So how are the guards?

Alar: Bunch of damned idiots. And I'm the chief idiot.

Thale: They made you Captain?

Alar: *(Gesturing to the throne.)* She made me Captain. I've become pretty damned efficient in these past three years.

Thale: I'm sorry.

Alar: Don't be. I'm here to arrest you.

Thale: Pardon?

(At the archway, Naotalba confronts Camilla, who is taking some air. She uses her Pallid Mask as a fan.)

Naotalba: Princess Camilla!

Camilla: Hello Naotalba. Is Thale here as well?

Naotalba: I understand these masks are due to you?

Camilla: Yes. The stranger wore one. Why?

Naotalba: The Pallid Mask is the face of the legendary herald of the King in Yellow.

Camilla: Then the stranger's brotherhood, they're friends of yours?

Naotalba: I have not heard of them.

Camilla: But they all wear these masks.

Naotalba: But the herald of the King in Yellow has a face like this, blank and white. His hands are soft, and cold like a corpse...

Camilla: Oh! You're always the same, aren't you? Is everything an omen?

Naotalba: During the end times, yes. Every action is an omen for those actions which follow. Where is this stranger?

Camilla: Oh, he'll be here. I'll let you know before he's presented to court. *(Suddenly.)* Oh! I see Thale at the balcony. Good night to you, Naotalba.

(Naotalba shakes his head sadly as Camilla goes to the balcony, arriving just prior to her next line. During the course of her walk she

is stopped many times by friends and suitors, with whom she animatedly chats.)

Alar: *(Conversationally.)* I've come to arrest you on your uncle's orders. He says that you accused him of treason or some damn thing. Against the law, you know, to accuse a prince of the blood of treason.

Thale: That didn't seem to be much of a problem last night when the guard arrested my brother.

Alar: How do you know about that?

Thale: I saw the whole thing. I saw Aldones dupe my poor, stupid sister into ordering it, and I saw the guard come to the courtyard. Has my uncle duped you as well? Or are you...

Alar: I'm just obeying the damned orders, Thale. So unless you slip away in the night again, which by the way you're entirely too damn good at, I'm taking you to the...

Thale: *(Coldly.)* There is more to being a soldier than cultivating the habit of obedience.

Alar: Thale, there haven't been any damned "soldiers" since we were children. We're called guards, Thale, because we guard the conquests of the past—and for as much damned money as gets thrown at us, it's pitiful how little we're actually paid. You know, five hundred years ago, the first King Thale conquered Hastur with an army half the size of the current guard...

Thale: *(Finally interrupting.)* That was a long time ago. Centuries.

Alar: Damn straight. My point is that the guards today have such overpriced and badly made equipment, so little pay, and so little love for this dynasty, that if you take away the "habit of obedience" they wouldn't have anything left at all.

(A pause.)

Thale: There's always hope, isn't there?

Camilla: *(Calling.)* Oh, Thale!

Thale: *(Turning with obvious relief.)* Camilla. How are you?

Camilla: *(Seeing Alar.)* I didn't realize you were with someone. I'll catch up later.

Thale and Alar:
(Eagerly, together.) No!

Thale: *(Somewhat calmer.)* No, by all means, stay. I believe you know Captain Alar?

Camilla: Oh dear.

Alar: *(Bowing.)* Princess Camilla.

Thale: *(To Camilla, conversationally.)* I'm surprised that Uoht isn't here. He usually enjoys all this dancing and capering about. Is he ill?

Camilla: *(Uncomfortable, she fidgets.)* Uoht is, ah, indisposed. No one seems to have seen him since dinner last night.

Thale: If no one has seen him...

(Thale, and indeed everyone in the room, is suddenly quiet and motionless, as if they had been frozen in ice for a moment. A gong

sounds dimly in the distance, and all continues as if nothing has happened.)

Thale: ...then how do you know that he's indisposed?

Camilla: Well, he must he indisposed if he isn't here, don't you think?

Thale: That's one theory.

Alar: And your theory is what?

Thale: Perhaps he's been detained. *(To Camilla.)* Perhaps he's even been arrested. Perhaps his dear, sweet sister...

Camilla: *(Aghast.)* I deny it!

Thale: ...has had him arrested on the orders of his unimpeachably honest uncle.

Alar: Thale, will you stop torturing the girl? *(To Camilla.)* He saw the whole damned thing, your majesty. Prince Aldones has sent me here to arrest him for it.

(As Camilla and Alar begin to argue, Thale slips away from them. By Alar's second line, he begins to chant the "Unseeing Eye".)

Camilla: You can't arrest Thale.

Alar: I beg your pardon? I was ordered to do so by a prince of the blood. Dammit, how can I *not* arrest him?

Camilla: But you love him. Or you did.

Alar: And you don't love your damned brother, Uoht?

Thale: *(Softly.)* Oodás horasa mae, gar esómí aorotos...

Camilla: I've never been very good at thinking things through. Thale thinks. And Uoht, well, he just *does* things... but of course I love them both. I love my brothers. But it's different.

Alar: Yes it is. I didn't choose to arrest the one I love. Or have you forgotten that it's your signature on that order?

Camilla: So you *do* love him!

Alar: *(Loudly.)* You signed a death warrant!

Camilla: Please! Keep your voice down. We mustn't let the Queen know.

Alar: Is that an order?

Camilla: It is.

Alar: You know, your majesty, I can remember when arrests were a matter of public record.

(Camilla begins to stare out of the window. She is obviously not listening to Alar.)

Alar: I can remember a time, and dammit it wasn't that long ago, when you needed an actual crime to arrest someone, not the suspicion that somebody might commit...

(Camilla walks to the window as if in a trance. EXIT Thale.)

Alar: Dammit, are you listening to me? Hello?
(Alar follows Camilla to the balcony window.)
Can you hear me? Are you all right?

Camilla: *(Distracted.)* Yes. Do... do you see it?

Alar: What? It seems a little dark tonight, but... say, you've got a damn funny way of changing the subject. You know, I've had just about enough of you. And your uncle. And Thale. *(Suddenly.)* Dammit! He did it again! Where...

Camilla: *(Interrupting.)* Go and see when the stranger is to be presented. Come back as soon as you know.

Alar: *(Shaking head in disbelief.)* Oh, absolutely your majesty.

(Alar walks to the arches and EXITS.)

Camilla: What is that there on the far shore?
No! *(Turns away from window.)*
No, a trick of the dying light.
(Turns back to window.)
Can I see it? No, I mustn't.
Can I deny my very sight?
I don't see those soaring towers.
I don't see those palace domes.
I deny it. I deny it. I deny it.

(A quiet, strobing light begins to shine on Camilla's face and she sing-songs to it's rhythm.)

Camilla: There is no city on the lake shore
Except Yhtill, our ancient home.
I deny those soaring towers,
I must disbelieve them still.
I deny those ancient domes,
There is no city but Yhtill!
I deny it; I deny it; I deny it!

(The strobing light ceases. Camilla shakes her head to clear it.)

(ENTER Alar. She walks to Camilla at the balcony.)

Camilla: All I ever wanted were a few distractions from the chore of living in these crazy times. All I ever wanted was to dance with lords and laugh with ladies and make it somehow through these times.

Alar: Your majesty?

Camilla: There is no city but Yhtill.

Alar: Your majesty, the stranger will be presented at eight.

Camilla: *(Awakening.)* I'm sorry. What?

Alar: The stranger will be presented at eight.

Camilla: What time is it now?

Alar: You have just a few moments, now.

Camilla: Thank you, Captain. That will be all.

(Alar, barely restraining her fury, salutes and walks to the table. Until she is found there by Aldones, she drinks. Naotalba finds Camilla at the balcony; she does not notice him until he touches her shoulder.)

Naotalba: I saw you at the window there, just now. Have you too seen Carcosa?

Camilla: *(Coldly.)* There is no city but Yhtill.

Naotalba: In that way, dear princess, sure madness lies. Can you doubt the evidence of your eyes?

Camilla: Naotalba, sometimes you must mistrust yourself.

Naotalba: As you wish. Have you seen Thale? He seems to have vanished.

Camilla: Thale's... gone on holiday.

Naotalba: Holiday?

Camilla: He's left the city. Where else is there for him to flee to now?

Naotalba: *(In disbelief.)* Nobody leaves the city. What is there to do outside the city? I cannot remember the last time someone left the city. And this stranger of yours...

(Naotalba, and indeed everyone in the room, is suddenly quiet and motionless, as if they had been frozen in ice for a moment. A gong sounds dimly in the distance, and all continues as if nothing has happened.)

Naotalba: ...is the first person to enter the city in...

Camilla: *(Interrupting.)* Oh! That reminds me!

Naotalba: What?

Camilla: The stranger. He'll be presented in just a few moments. You asked me to let you know.

Naotalba: Thank you. Yes. Let us see if he is indeed the Pallid Mask. Let us see if it's a mask or a face.

Camilla: Really, Naotalba. Only you would think that was his face.

(ENTER Bremchas. He walks to the throne. Cassilda is sitting there; she has removed her mask. Bremchas is not wearing a mask.)

Bremchas: Your majesty, an ambassador craves audience. He hails from a foreign world where his king righteously reigns. He has come to our world...

(Bremchas, and indeed everyone in the room, is suddenly quiet and motionless, as if they had been frozen in ice for a moment. A gong dimly sounds in the distance, and all continues as if nothing has happened.)

Bremchas: ...of Hastur, to our city of Yhtill, to present himself to your majesty's court.

Cassilda: Pray admit him.

(Bremchas bows to his Queen and EXITS. He ENTERS a moment later, with the Stranger following him. As he leads the Stranger to the throne, the crowd quietly turns to face them. Bremchas presents the Stranger, bows to Cassilda, and moves to stand beside the throne.)

Stranger: *(In a voice only slightly less grating than before.)*
A message from my king have I.

Cassilda: We shall be delighted to receive it.

Stranger: It a message for all is.

Cassilda: By all means, let us hear it.

(A silence falls upon the expectant crowd. A gong sounds dimly in the distance and the Stranger recites, during which time his voice becomes more and more human. During this speech, the instruments in the band play soft, randomly ascending scales.)

Stranger: Hunts and eats the gods the dead King.
Darkened are skies,
Tremble the bones of the earth-god,
Stilled the planets are, and,
And the Hyades made cold.
For they have seen the King

>   Appearing in his power,
>   As a god who on his fathers lives
>   And on his mothers feeds.
>   A master of wisdom is the King.
>   The glory of the King is in the sky,
>   His power is in the horizon,
>   Forever rooted in the stones.

(By this point, the Stranger's voice is nearly human.)

Stranger: The dead King hunts and eats the gods.
> The skies are darkened,
> The bones of the earth-god tremble,
> The planets are stilled, and
> The Hyades made cold.
> For they have seen the King
> Appearing in his power,
> The dead King who hunts and eats the world.

(There is a confused moment of silence, and then pandemonium ensues as the guests attempt to make sense of this utterance.)

Aldones: He is a creature of the priests!

Naotalba: *(Triumphantly throwing his hands into the air.)* He is the herald of the King!

(Aldones seeks out Alar, and they converse in low tones while Naotalba and Camilla speak.)

Camilla: *(To Naotalba in disbelief.)* No... No! I am not mad. I am not mad. I don't believe you. I *won't* believe you.

Naotalba: *(Grinning.)* You have heard him—how can you deny it?

Camilla: I deny it. You're hallucinating. You're all just crazy.

(Camilla walks away, heading for the throne.)

Aldones: *(Through his teeth.)* Those are your orders, Captain. The stranger is not to leave this hall except in your custody.

Alar: Yes, my lord.

Aldones: And I want the city searched. Thale couldn't have gotten far. Naotalba, I shall deal with myself.

Alar: Yes, my lord.

(EXIT Aldones. Alar moves to the side of the throne opposite of Bremchas. Cassilda leads the Stranger to the table with Camilla following.)

Cassilda: That was very... unusual. Your, ah, voice seems to be improving.

Stranger: The alignment proceeds.

Cassilda: *(Suddenly.)* Would you care for a drink?

Stranger: Thirsty am... I am thirsty. *(He drinks.)*

Camilla: *(Arriving.)* Mother!

Cassilda: Oh there you are Camilla. Have you seen either of your brothers lately?

Camilla: Ah... Thale was here.

Cassilda: Yes, I saw him earlier; is he still here? And have you seen Uoht?

Stranger: *(Turning to Camilla.)*
The Yellow Sign found you have?

>   The Yellow Sign you found have?
>   The Yellow Sign have you found?

Camilla: (*Incredulous. Panicked.*) What?

Stranger: Have you found the Yellow Sign?
Have you found the Yellow Sign?
Have you found the Yellow Sign?

Camilla: What? No. I haven't seen anything. I haven't found anything. I feel... feel...

(*An uncomfortable pause as the Stranger stares at Camilla, who begins to shiver. She hugs herself in an effort to keep warm.*)

Cassilda: (*Suddenly.*) Would you like something to eat?

Stranger: I hunger. (*He eats.*)

Cassilda: (*Pulling Camilla aside.*) What was that all about?

Camilla: I... I don't know. He's so very strange. Listen, I need to tell you something. I was trying to help, I only ever made one decision, but everything's gone all wrong, and I feel like I'm losing my mind.

Cassilda: Oh, dear, the party's just fine. It's true the stranger is a little odd, and his hands—so cold, but he is...

Camilla: It's not about the party. It's Uoht...

Cassilda: Have you seen him?

Camilla: Have I seen him?

Cassilda: (*Confused.*) Yes, what...

(Cassilda, and indeed everyone in the room except the Stranger, is suddenly quiet and motionless, as if they had been frozen in ice for a moment. A gong dimly sounds in the distance, and all continues.)

Cassilda: *(Slowly and with great confusion.)* What... what was that?

Camilla: *(Eyes wide, shaking.)* You felt it too?

(The Stranger, who stops eating, stands between Cassilda and Camilla.)

Stranger: The alignment of the spheres is imminent. I am the catalyst for all that was foreseen. The end approaches.

Cassilda: I beg your pardon?

Camilla: *(Shaking.)* I can't stand it!

(Bremchas moves to the front of the throne.)

Bremchas: *(Announcing grandly.)* Your majesties, lords, and ladies! The hour of truth is at hand! The appointed time has come to reveal yourselves. Unmask and discover with whom you have been dancing!

(Some slight and scattered applause. Bremchas moves back into position next to the throne. As the guests drop their masks, they murmur sounds of approval, disapproval, surprise, and laughter. Camilla hesitates a moment before dropping her mask. She forces a smile. The Stranger does not move.)

Camilla: You, sir, should unmask.

Stranger: Indeed?

Cassilda: Indeed, it's time. We all have laid aside disguise but you.

Stranger: I wear no mask.

Camilla: *(Terrified, aside to Cassilda.)* No mask? No mask!

Cassilda: *(Wonderment.)* I think he speaks the truth.

Stranger: I am truth.

Camilla: *(Shrieks, loudly.)* You've all gone crazy! You're crazy! The world's coming undone—oh, why won't you leave me alone? *(Increasingly hysterical.)* Signs and cities not there and that, that *thing* with no face, and dark stars and, and... *(Breaks down, sobbing.)* You're all crazy, and you're making me crazy, too!

Stranger: Mark these words, for they shall echo through the streets outside forever, when they are Carcosa's streets. There is no liberation. There is no end. There is no future...

Camilla: *(An agonized scream.)* No!

(CURTAIN)

Act II, Scene I

The Torturer's chamber in the Dhooric Tower. The room is shadowy and indistinct, but large and obscure pieces of machinery are scattered about the chamber. There is a rack and a press at left and a heavy wooden doorway at center right. To the right is a large cabinet. Its doors are ajar, revealing various whips and other implements hanging inside. Downstage right is a small desk and a stool.

The door squeaks slightly as it opens. The entire place is thick with dust and decay.

(ENTER Aldones and Cassilda.)

Aldones: The prisoners must be tortured to death.

Cassilda: 'Tis a long time indeed since this chamber has been used. Even father rarely used it. He never spoke of it; I think it embarrassed him.

(Aldones takes a whip from the cabinet. He fidgets idly with it for the remainder of the scene.)

Aldones: Ah, but he ruled Yhtill, indeed all of Hastur, firmly and without opposition. Even you can see that firm action must be taken if the power of the priesthood is to be ended. This stranger is their puppet. Poor Camilla has been driven out of her mind. Thale is one of them now, and Uoht has vanished. They are attempting to destroy our dynasty.

Cassilda: I know it.

Aldones: Then do something about it. You have been far too lax for far too long, dear sister; you must crush them utterly. You must send to them a clear sign that you are in command here, not Naotalba. We

Cassilda: cannot have the rabble flocking to the priests. You must be firm.

Cassilda: We cannot enter into the temple to arrest them. What would you have me do?

Aldones: We can crush their will to resist. We can show them, by the death of all of the prisoners here now, that we mean to stay in power.

Cassilda: You lecture me like Naotalba. Everything is a symbol.

Aldones: Our words may be similar, but he and I have far different ends in view. He wishes to subvert our dynasty...

Cassilda: *(Interrupting.)* And you?

Aldones: ...in order to hasten the reign of his ridiculous god. As if any god would allow Naotalba to rule Yhtill.

Cassilda: So what is the danger of him?

Aldones: He incites the rabble against us. And he knows that we haven't the soldiers—or the will to use them—to restore order. His kind thrives in chaos and uncertainty. We must save our future from his future.

Cassilda: Always the future. What about now?

Aldones: Send them a sign. Show them that our dynasty still has power and the will to use it.

Cassilda: You say that I must torture all of the prisoners to death.

Aldones: I do.

Cassilda: And this stranger—this Pallid Mask—what is his role?

Aldones: *(Hesitates.)* I don't know, and that is why we must question him. We must learn Naotalba's plans, and this stranger must be his ally.

Cassilda: *(Resigned.)* You are right, of course. It must be done.

Aldones: It must be done.

Cassilda: Your selfless advice, Aldones, has aided me tremendously these past days.

Aldones: Thank you, my queen. It is my duty to aid the crown when I can.

Cassilda: A lesser man would be bitter that I were Queen at all. I shall conduct the stranger's questioning myself.

Aldones: *(Clearly shocked.)* You? But I...

Cassilda: *(Firmly.)* No. I have studied the ancient uses where you have not. You shall see that the rest of the prisoners are put to death. Have the stranger sent here. Now.

Aldones: *(Biting.)* Yes, my queen.

(EXIT Aldones.)

Cassilda: Now we shall find the truth. Aldones plots as much as Naotalba, and between them I am in a vise. I doubt this stranger knows much, but he disturbs me, and I must see what Aldones plans. I must give them each enough rope to fashion their own nooses. Perhaps Aldones knows this stranger better than he says—I shall discover that as well, if I may.

Aldones has always talked of empire, but since we were children all we have had has been the city. Do not the prophesies of old speak of twelve monarchs? Do they not say that the last would be overthrown in shame and then followed by a dreaded thirteenth "Last King?" Am I not the twelfth of our dynasty to sit upon Yhtill's dragon throne? All I had ever wanted was to survive, to prove them wrong, to somehow break the curse put on our family long ago, and both Aldones and Naotalba seem determined that prophecy be carried out, even if Aldones does it unwittingly and Naotalba does it witlessly.

But I will survive and prove them all wrong. I will subvert the destiny others choose for me, but I must be careful. I mustn't allow Naotalba to remind the people of prophecy.

(The door opens.)

Cassilda: But here must be the prisoner.

(ENTER Bicree and Bremchas, leading the Stranger in chains.)

Cassilda: Tie him down. We shall soften him up a little first. Prepare him for the cat.

(Bremchas removes the Stranger's robe, revealing simple, grey garments beneath. Bremchas carefully hangs the robe upon a peg near the door. The embroidered Yellow Sign upon it is clearly visible.)

(Bicree fastens the Stranger's wrists into cuffs with a rope attached. He throws the rope over a beam, draws the Stranger's arms fully over his head, and ties off the rope. Cassilda takes a cat 'o nine tails from the cabinet.)

Cassilda: I cannot bear the sight of his head. Cover it. Private, will you serve us as scribe?

Bremchas: With pleasure, my Queen.

(Bicree finds an execution hood—a burlap sack—which he places over the Stranger's head. Bremchas sits himself at the small desk to right. He takes paper and pen and writes down everything said during the questioning.)

Cassilda: I have no desire to disregard the ancient forms, for although our grandfathers were better taught the Torturer's ways, you should not suffer from our lack of education. I have read widely and deeply in the library below us, and I shall do my best to conduct these proceedings according to the ancient and accepted procedures.

Stranger: Your diligence honours me.

Cassilda: Very well, let us begin. You will answer my questions. If you do not answer them to my satisfaction, you will be punished. Do you understand?

Stranger: I do.

Bremchas: *(Repeating as he writes.)* I do.

(This dialogue should build, slowly and methodically, faster and more desperate on Cassilda's part, and louder and firmer on the Stranger's part, until Cassilda throws up her hands in frustration.)

Cassilda: We shall begin simply. What is your name? *(A pause.)* Your name?

Stranger: I am truth.

Cassilda: *(She whips him.)* Let's try again, shall we? What is your name?

Stranger: I am truth.

Cassilda: *(She whips him.)* What is your name?

Stranger: Can you not accept the truth?

Cassilda: Mind your tongue. *(She whips him.)* What is the truth?

Stranger: I am truth.

Cassilda: *(She whips him.)* What is your name?

Stranger: Can you not accept the truth?

Cassilda: What is truth?

Stranger: I am truth.

Cassilda: Oh, we're getting nowhere.

Stranger: We are trapped, you and I. You are locked into this tower and into this chamber just as surely as I am.

Cassilda: What is your relationship with Naotalba?

Stranger: I have never met Naotalba.

Cassilda: *(She whips him.)* Do you serve the priests?

Stranger: The truth serves all who know it, but the priests do not serve me.

Cassilda: The truth is all I seek. Why will you not submit?

Stranger: I am truth; I submit to no one.

Cassilda: *(She whips him.)* What is your name?

(A milky white fluid begins to ooze from the tatters on the Stranger's whipped back.)

Stranger: Sadness leaks from this phantom's body, as faceless truth...

Cassilda: *(Her words punctuated by the whip upon the Stranger's back.)* Enough! Answer the question!

Stranger: *(Pained.)* Can you not accept the truth?

Cassilda: What is truth?

Stranger: I am truth.

Cassilda: Bah! *(Throws up arms in disgust, fairly screaming in her frustration and rage.)*

(A pause. Cassilda rubs her eyes.)

Cassilda: *(Calmer now.)* All right. All right. Guards, press him.

(Bicree and Bremchas let the Stranger down and put him into a machine similar to a wine-press, but vertical instead of horizontal. There is a large wheel-shaped screw on the machine.)

(Bicree turns the wheel three times. He stands ready at the wheel and turns it on Cassilda's command. Bremchas returns to the desk.)

Bicree: We stand ready, your majesty.

Bremchas: *(Gravely.)* Indeed, your majesty; the truth awaits.

Cassilda: Thank you, gentlemen. *(To Stranger.)* You will answer my questions. If you do not answer them

	to my satisfaction, you will be punished. Do you understand?
Stranger:	I do.
Cassilda:	I think we shall begin a new line of questioning. Since the truth appears so elusive, let us instead inquire after the facts.
Bremchas:	*(Repeating as he writes.)* The facts.
Stranger:	It is ordained that you would not recognize truth after so many lifetimes of dissimilitude.
Cassilda:	I know the truth.
Stranger:	But not *for* truth. I am but a phantom to you. And so it is.
Cassilda:	Turn the screw, Corporal. You make no sense.
Stranger:	Because you no longer sense truth.
Cassilda:	Facts, not truth, is what we seek now. I tire of this dance. Tell me Naotalba's plans.
Stranger:	The fact, then, is that Naotalba's plans, and those of Aldones, and those of all of the rest, are irrelevant to their destiny.
Cassilda:	And what is their destiny, oh prophet?
Stranger:	*(Simply.)* They shall die.
Cassilda:	*(Angry.)* Turn the screw. Your banal pronouncements do not frighten me. I want facts.
Stranger:	Truth is not meant to frighten. It exists in utter indifference to human action, emotion, or thought. Truth is perceived, not created.

Cassilda: *(Angry.)* Turn the screw. Facts! Why did your voice change?

Stranger: When I arrived I was out of phase. The alignment is now nearly complete and Yhtill exists no more.

Cassilda: Turn the screw. Facts! Where are you from?

Stranger: I have journeyed from Carcosa to Carcosa, pausing only a short time at forgotten Yhtill, until it left me.

Cassilda: Turn the screw. Facts! Who are you?

(A dull, crunching noise. A milky white fluid begins to leak from around the Stranger's crushed chest.)

Stranger: *(Groans.)* I... truth am I.

Cassilda: *(Angry.)* Even now, you gibber. Rack him! Rack him!

(Bicree and Bremchas spin the screw to release the Stranger. His clothing is damp with a white, milky substance. He collapses and is carried to and placed upon the rack without resistance or protest of any kind. Bicree ties the Stranger's limbs to the rack and turns the screw three times. Bremchas returns to the desk.)

(During the course of the following dialogue, occasional screaming and wailing is heard from other chambers in the tower. These should start out fairly innocuously, and should build in intensity and volume, culminating in Uoht's death scream.)

Cassilda: You are not "truth," whatever that may be. You are my prisoner, and you will answer the questions. The scratch of the cat, the agony of the press, are as nothing to the rack. Every turn of that screw will be a hundred demons, pulling apart the very fibres of your body.

Stranger: *(Weakly.)* As you wish.

Bremchas: *(Repeats as he writes.)* As you wish.

Cassilda: You will answer my questions. If you do not answer them to my satisfaction, you will be punished. Do you understand?

Stranger: I do.

Cassilda: Since you seem to know so little about yourself, tell me about Naotalba.

Stranger: I know less about Naotalba.

Cassilda: Turn the screw. Tell me what you know. Why does he call you the Pallid Mask?

Stranger: *(With difficulty.)* Truth is formless...

Cassilda: Nebulous, you mean. Turn the screw. What has happened to your brotherhood? They have vanished from the palace.

Stranger: It is as you say. They were a hundred half-truths now irrelevant.

Cassilda: Turn the screw. That wheel will turn until you are shreds, if you do not give me some useful answers soon. Why does Aldones hate you so? Surely you cannot be ignorant of that?

(The Stranger relates his parable without stopping for Cassilda's numerous interruptions. Cassilda's lines should be spoken over the parable, to which she is attempting not to listen.)

Stranger: Two proud brothers shared a house. Their family, once wealthy, was now quite poor, and they

	owned but one jar for water, one jar for grain, their old house, and a dog.
Cassilda:	What? What are you talking about?
Stranger:	One day, the dog accidentally knocked over a lantern, causing a small fire. The two proud brothers fell to arguing over...
Cassilda:	Stop that. Be quiet.
Stranger:	...who was worthier to put out the flame, for there was but one jar for water. And while they argued, the fire grew, until it consumed the one jar for grain. And still...
Cassilda:	Be quiet I say. I don't care about jars or fires. Answer my questions.
Stranger:	...they argued, until the fires grew and consumed their entire house. In their haste to flee, the two proud brothers...
Cassilda:	*(Loudly.)* Be quiet! Are you listening to me? Quiet!
Stranger:	...dropped their one jar for water, and it too was consumed by the now raging fire. Saddened and angered by...
Cassilda:	*(Shouting.)* Stop it! Quiet I say! Turn the screw, Corporal, shut him up!
Stranger:	...the loss of their one jar for grain, and their one jar for water, and their house, all of which were burnt to ashes, the two proud brothers resolved at length...
Cassilda:	*(Screams.)* Quiet!

THE KING IN YELLOW

Stranger: ...to kill their dog.

(Silence. A pause.)

Cassilda: *(Calmer.)* There.

Stranger: I am finished.

(Cassilda takes a few deep breaths. During the next exchange, she becomes louder and angrier until at last she takes the screw herself. She barely waits for the Stranger's responses before asking a new question. Bicree turns the screw after each answer.)

Cassilda: Turn the screw, and keep it turning. You tell me tales, which are lies: every fiction is a lie. Tell me facts, damn you. What have you done to Camilla?

Stranger: Has she not two other parts to play?

Cassilda: Where is Thale?

Stranger: Is he not sunk into a darkness of his own design?

Cassilda: Where is Uoht?

Stranger: Is he not...

(Uoht's dying scream loudly echoes through the chamber, interrupting the Stranger. A pause.)

Cassilda: *(Teeth gritted.)* Where is Uoht?

Stranger: *(Sadly.)* You have killed him.

Cassilda: No! I deny it. How dare you accuse me, how dare you! We have been far too gentle in the face of your lies! Have you foreseen this...?

(Cassilda grabs the screw and savagely turns it, again and again, until a hideous tearing noise causes her to pause. She takes her hands off of the screw and stands back, clearly shocked.)

Stranger: *(Dully.)* So this is how you slay truth. Was it not inevitable from the beginning that the end should come? But I am only a phantom, so your crime lies only in the revealing, not in the murder.

(The Stranger's hands tear off of his arms at the ropes which bind them. A white milky substance dribbles out, and the Stranger's arms fall limply to his sides.)

Stranger: I am already dead. Even you must have seen that.

Cassilda: *(Angry, incredulous.)* Still you will not submit?

(Bicree takes a backward step. A pause. Bremchas puts down his paper, walks to the rack, and gently touches the Stranger's oozing wrist.)

Bremchas: He is dead, your majesty.

Cassilda: *(Mocking, coming down off of her anger.)* Is truth so easily dispatched?

Bicree: *(Shaking.)* Perhaps all is not well with the world, your majesty, if creatures such as this are permitted to walk upon it.

Bremchas: *(Releasing the Stranger's wrist.)* What shall we do now, your majesty?

Cassilda: I don't know. *(A pause.)* Dispose of the body.

Bremchas: It... it seems to be melting away.

Cassilda: What?

(The door suddenly slams open. ENTER Camilla. She is very pale and is wearing a white nightgown, which should be a shocking contrast to the griminess of the chamber. She appears almost ethereal or angelic.)

(Her manner is disoriented and distant; her gaze keeps wandering. She is oblivious to her surroundings.)

Cassilda: Camilla! What are you doing out of bed? What are you doing up here?

Camilla: I don't know. I got up to... to... look for something.

Cassilda: *(Gently.)* Well, it's not up here, dear. Go back down to your rooms.

Camilla: The city's gone. Carcosa's gone.

Cassilda: What?

Camilla: It just... disappeared. It's not there. Everything's... different. The gates are... shut... shut against them.

Cassilda: You're not well dear. Go downstairs.

(Cassilda motions to Bicree, who takes Camilla gently by the arm and begins leading her back to the door.)

Cassilda: This nice man here will take you back to your rooms. Everything will be just fine.

Camilla: They're not my rooms. I feel so... so strange. *(Brightening suddenly, grabbing up the Stranger's robe.)* Oh! Here it is!

Cassilda: Camilla?

Camilla: *(Hugging the robe joyfully to her face, sobbing.)*
Here it is.
I've found it.
I've found it.
I've found it.

Cassilda: *(Frightened.)* What? What is it? Are you all right?

Camilla: *(Pulling away from Bicree and holding up the robe to Cassilda.)* Don't you see it? I've found it. I've found it.

Cassilda: What? What have you found?

Camilla: *(Showing Cassilda.)* Don't you see I've found the Yellow Sign? It was here all the time. It was on him all the time. Don't you see I've found the Yellow Sign? Don't you know what this means?

(Bicree faints; Bremchas hangs his head in despair.)

Cassilda: Camilla, I...

Camilla: *(Shouting.)* Joy! Great joy! For I have found the Yellow Sign!

Cassilda: Camilla! That's enough, we can't let them know!

Camilla: Everyone will know! *(Laughs, wide-eyed.)* What does it matter? Let them know! *(Turns, and shouts out the door.)* Joy! Great joy! For I have found the Yellow Sign!

Cassilda: *(Shouting.)* That's enough!

Camilla: *(Turns to her mother. Small. Her voice mocks in sadness and fear.)* Oh, will you kill me, too?

(A pause. Cassilda opens her mouth, speechless. Camilla turns back to the door and marches out, shouting with joy.)

Camilla: *(Shouting.)* Joy! Great joy! For I have found the Yellow Sign! The end is come!

(CURTAIN)

Act II, Scene II

The great hall. Outside the balcony, no stars are to be seen, though the sky is black. Carcosa has vanished. Bremchas and Bicree sit upon the steps before the throne. Bremchas is eating a pear.

Bicree: The Queen is deep in mourning.

Bremchas: *(Munching.)* Aye, hysterical she is. One moment calm, the next maddened. Still, it was she who ordered all the prisoners killed. *(Throws remains of pear behind him.)* Darn shame about Prince Uoht, really.

Bicree: How could she not know?

Bremchas: *(Picking his teeth.)* Well, she knows now. And then there's the matter of Carcosa.

Bicree: Not Carcosa again. Always it's Carcosa. What now?

Bremchas: *(Looks suspiciously about and then whispers conspiratorially.)* It's vanished!

Bicree: Bremchas, you idiot, it was never there to begin with.

Bremchas: Aye, possibly, but it's here now.

Bicree: What are...

Guard One: *(Off stage, distant.)* Make way for the Queen!

(Bremchas and Bicree rush to either side of the throne, where they snap to attention. ENTER Cassilda and Aldones. Cassilda wears a black mourning dress, and Aldones has a black sash across his usual fine and meticulous dress.)

Aldones: We must be strong, my Queen, in our adversity. Tragedy must temper us to hard, intractable steel.

Cassilda: *(Sobbing.)* My son is dead. Uoht is dead. And 'twas my order that killed him! My order!

(Cassilda collapses, sobbing, into the throne.)

Aldones: To be scrupulously fair, sister, it was Camilla's order that sent him to the tower. It is she who is responsible.

Cassilda: But 'twas I who ordered the prisoners to their deaths.

Aldones: Upon my suggestion. It was a reasonable and prudent course of action...

Cassilda: *(Wails.)* Reasonable!

Aldones: *(Firmly.)* Reasonable. Neither you nor I could know that Camilla had...

Cassilda: I don't deserve to live.

Aldones: Who amongst us does?

Bremchas: *(Brightly.)* I do!

(Bicree turns sharply to Bremchas in surprise. Cassilda and Aldones ignore the outburst.)

Cassilda: Uoht deserved to live, deserved a life, and I killed him!

Aldones: Surely it was Camilla who killed him, as surely as if she had done it with her own hands. She is a traitor; don't let the fact that she's your daughter blind you to that.

Cassilda: Tread carefully, Aldones. 'Tis true; she is my only daughter, and with Thale in the priesthood she stands to inherit the throne.

Aldones: Exactly your majesty. She is in league with Naotalba to seize the throne.

Cassilda: Naotalba...? But 'tis Thale who serves the priesthood.

Aldones: And is it not a cunning plan? Naotalba knows that Thale is far too intelligent to manipulate so readily, so he makes him a priest to keep him from the throne. Uoht is, that is, he *was* too impulsive and short tempered to ever make a successful servant. But Camilla, sweet emotional, superficial Camilla, would make the perfect priestly puppet. Honey-tongued Naotalba could convince her of anything.

Cassilda: It has the ring of truth to it.

Aldones: I have thought long on the matter.

Cassilda: *(Dismissive.)* But she is mad now. She could never be queen.

Aldones: Perhaps, her uses through, Naotalba has discarded her. Perhaps he means to seize the throne himself.

Cassilda: *(Deeply suspicious.)* If a priest could be king, 'Twould be Thale, rather than Naotalba, who is not even a member of our dynasty. Or perhaps 'twill be you, Aldones. Perhaps we could insert your name into the litany of conspiracy and treason?

Aldones: I am as honest as Uoht! Bring Naotalba here! Ask him of his treason and his...

Cassilda: *(Coldly.)* Since the deaths in the tower he will not leave the temple. Shall we then invite him to leave his sanctuary of his own accord? Or shall we just break the law and drag him here by force?

Aldones: Your majesty is the law.

Cassilda: No. I enforce it. I can make it. But it is not me.

Aldones: Then alter the law. Is not the survival of our dynasty the highest law?

(A pause.)

Cassilda: I cannot do it.

Aldones: Think of Uoht.

(A pause.)

Cassilda: Sanctuary is the oldest law.

Aldones: Change it. These are new times.

(A pause.)

Cassilda: *(Sadly resigned.)* You are right, of course. What does it matter?

Aldones: *(To Bicree.)* Bring me Naotalba. Take a squad of men into the temple, Corporal, and bring him out.

Bicree: Yes, my lord. Shall I inform the Captain, my lord?

Aldones: *(To Bremchas.)* Private, go and inform the Captain.

Bremchas: *(Enthusiastically.)* Yes my lord!

(Bremchas and Bicree salute and EXIT.)

Aldones: Now we shall see how the Priest answers for his crimes.

(A pause.)

Cassilda: 'Tis cold.

Aldones: It is, rather. Unseasonable.

(A pause.)

Cassilda: *(Simultaneous.)* You know I...

Aldones: *(Simultaneous.)* I'm sorry about... oh.

Cassilda: After you.

Aldones: I'm sorry about Uoht. I do grieve for him, and I'm... I'm...

Cassilda: Thank you. And thank you for your counsel. I don't know what I would have done without it.

Aldones: It has been a difficult time. *(A pause.)* What did you learn from the stranger?

Cassilda: Nothing of use.

Aldones: I'll read the transcript. Was there anything in his manner...

Cassilda: *(Interrupting.)* What does it matter? He is vanished as if he never existed. And poor, sweet Camilla...

Naotalba: *(Interrupting from offstage, indignantly.)* Unhand me, I say! I can walk.

Aldones: Now we shall see.

(Aldones swirls to the side of the throne. ENTER Alar, Naotalba, Bicree, and Bremchas, in a line. Bremchas and Bicree have their muskets in hand; Alar is unarmed. She is not wearing her hat. Bremchas moves to the side of the throne opposite Aldones while Bicree stands by the door. They do not shoulder their muskets.)

Naotalba: *(Raging.)* Your majesty presumes too much! I have right of sanctuary! I am High Priest, not some skulking cutpurse! You have no right, no right at all, to pull me from my temple, and under armed guard. You have no right to...

Alar: *(Loudly interrupting.)* Quiet, dammit! Let's get this straightened out. *(Politely, to Cassilda.)* Did your majesty order this arrest?

Aldones: She did.

Alar: Is your majesty aware that the right of temple sanctuary is protected by the law?

Aldones: The law has been altered.

Alar: *(To Aldones.)* Dammit, you can't just change the law on a whim! The law's the law.

Aldones: The Queen has altered the law. It was necessary and rational that this be done.

Alar: *(To Cassilda.)* Does Prince Aldones speak for your majesty?

Cassilda: He does. We have ordered Naotalba's arrest ourself. 'Tis for the protection of the dynasty we do it.

Alar: *(Incredulously.)* Protection of the...? Dammit, that's...

Aldones: *(Interrupting.)* That's enough, Captain. Silence.

Alar: But you can't just...

Aldones: I said that's enough.

Alar: *(Turning and muttering.)* The habit of obedience wears thin.

Aldones: Now, Naotalba, your infamous plan is revealed to us.

Naotalba: *(Somewhat calmed down.)* Aldones, you old liar, what are you talking about? Are you the one who convinced the Queen to violate the law?

Aldones: The Queen's majesty makes her own decisions. We accuse you of plotting the murder of Prince Uoht and of conspiring to overthrow our government. How do you plead?

Naotalba: *(Whistles.)* Well, I am impressed. Me? Killing Uoht?

Aldones: *(Firmly.)* How do you plead?

Naotalba: *(To Cassilda.)* Your majesty, this is patently ridiculous. It is not me who plots, but Aldones. Camilla will tell you the truth, if you will but ask her.

Aldones: Camilla is conveniently out of her mind at the moment. Do you insult us by denying the charges?

Naotalba: You are quite a work, Aldones. Why should I possibly want to overthrow your dynasty? It is the

	end times, and soon the King in Yellow will arrive and institute his reign of the righteous.
Aldones:	With you, no doubt, as its leader.
Naotalba:	If it should please him.
Aldones:	*(To Cassilda.)* You see? He admits his treason.
Naotalba:	*(To Cassilda.)* Your majesty, I am merely repeating the dogma of the church, as it was in your father's time, and in his mother's time, and all the way back to the time of the first King Thale. The prophecy of Hali...
Aldones:	*(Interrupting.)* Traitor! You plot to...
Cassilda:	*(Interrupting.)* 'Tis enough, Aldones, let him finish.
Naotalba:	*(Bows.)* Thank you, your majesty. I was just going to remind your majesty that your dynasty rules because it is the will of our god that it do so. Hali prophesied a time when it would be the will of our god to manifest himself as the King in Yellow and rule directly. That time now fast approaches. I have no need to overthrow anyone.
Cassilda:	Aldones?
Aldones:	*(To Naotalba.)* You say that our dynasty rules by the will of a god, but is it not obvious that we rule Yhtill because we choose to? We are strong; we have will, regardless of what Naotalba here thinks. We have will, and it is our will that we rule Yhtill, not the will of some mythical god.
Naotalba:	You again succumb to your erroneous belief that rationalization is real. The world is not such a rational place.

Aldones: How can anyone be so profoundly wrong?

Cassilda: *(Ignoring Aldones.)* What, then, is the cause of our government?

Naotalba: To serve the will of our god.

Aldones: To serve the will of our dynasty.

Naotalba: The gods will not be denied!

Cassilda: And what of the people's will?

(A distant gong sounds, and shouts are heard in the distance.)

Aldones: What?

Bremchas: Yak's nipples!

(ENTER Thale. His clothes are torn, and his eyes are blind, bleeding sores. He staggers into the room, hands feeling his way before him.)

Thale: *(Disoriented.)* I go from the city gate and look before me, and I see only mounds and tombs and...

(General sounds of shock and dismay are heard from all, interrupting Thale and silencing him.)

Cassilda: *(Simultaneous, greatly disturbed.)* What happened...

Naotalba: *(Simultaneous, concerned, confused.)* Where have you been...

Cassilda and Naotalba:
    (Together.) ...my son?

Alar: Oh Thale, what happened?

Thale: I see behind the veil of the world, and it makes me blind.

Alar: But what did you see? And your eyes! Your...

Thale: A battle flag, outside the city gates. Smoke ascends from the faded and ragged banner, and the sound of musketry and cannon comes faintly like a dream of an echo heard in a tomb. It is the last thing I see.

Cassilda: Where did he go? Where did he go?

Alar: He left the city.

Cassilda: Left the city? But why?

Alar: He was running from me... again. You think he'd learn.

Cassilda: But Thale, what happened to your eyes?

Naotalba: *(In wonderment.)* Like the first king, Prince Thale is blinded. A miracle!

Cassilda: But who did this? Who is responsible?

Thale: Ask Naotalba. Ask him. Why has Carcosa vanished? And to where? Why are friends long dead walking through our streets? Whence comes the army at our very gates? Ask the High Priest— you have him here mother, ask him—for the secret of it is *he does not know!*

You small-minded so-called leaders of a withering empire plot and plan for the future in here and all the while, outside your cozy little battlemented walls, the future is happening. I could not bear the awful beauty now outside the gates. *(Sobs.)*

	I couldn't bear it anymore. Our world is tired to death, and all of the creatures in it.
Alar:	I'm not tired, Thale. I'm not tired anymore; I've just been alone, playing the part, wearing the mask, for so long.
Thale:	*(Finds Alar.)* Centuries, my love. I'll not leave again.
Alar:	Dammit Thale…
Thale:	*(Collapsing into Alar's arms, he sobs.)* I'm so afraid…
Alar:	I do love you, you damned idiot.
Aldones:	This goes far enough. Captain, arrest him.
Alar:	No, my lord.
Aldones:	What?
Alar:	I refuse, my lord. I am no longer blind and in the habit of obedience.
Cassilda:	*(To Aldones.)* Do you propose to arrest my only living son? I should have sent you to the chamber.
Aldones:	Apparently not. No, no of course not. But the Captain here has proved herself… disobedient.
Thale:	*(Stands.)* Better disobedient than disloyal.
Cassilda:	What does that mean? *(Silence.)* And you, Aldones. Honestly, you make even less sense than Thale some days.
Naotalba:	Pay no mind. The end is at hand.

Thale:	*(To Aldones.)* The end is here, uncle, and nothing you do postpones it in any way.
Aldones:	*(To Cassilda.)* You see? You see? You should arrest him—he is just another tool of the priesthood.
Thale:	*(To Naotalba.)* The end is here, reverend father, and nothing you do hastens it in any way.
Aldones:	What more evidence to you need? Arrest them both!
Alar:	Arrest yourself. *(To Thale.)* Come with me. Let's get out of the city while we can.
Thale:	What is the point of running? Of fleeing? We cannot escape Carcosa. We cannot now save ourselves, and I doubt we ever could.
Alar:	There is always hope. Didn't you tell me that once?
Thale:	I lied. Or I didn't know. Truth is just a phantom anyway.
Alar:	If... if I leave the city, will you come with me?
Thale:	*(Shrugs.)* In the end...
Alar:	*(Insistent.)* Will you?
Thale:	In the end, it doesn't matter what we do.
Alar:	Come with me, then.

(Alar leads Thale to the arches. Aldones begins to pursue them.)

Cassilda:	Let them go.

(Bremchas restrains Aldones. Alar and Thale EXIT.)

Cassilda: Let them go. Perhaps they can save themselves.

Aldones: *(Shrugs.)* They're walking to their deaths out there. Am I the only rational one here?

Naotalba: Carcosa. The Yellow Sign. You never saw.

Aldones: *(Sharply.)* You still don't. The future belongs to me.

Naotalba: The future is ours!

Cassilda: Gentlemen, gentlemen, can we not put the future behind us for a moment?

Aldones: Behind? Behind? *(Laughs uproariously, into tears.)*

Cassilda: *(Shocked.)* Aldones! *(A pause while Aldones continues to laugh.)* Aldones! Are you all right?

Aldones: *(Serious again.)* I had wanted to laugh earlier, but I was too busy.

(A pause.)

Cassilda: You're a fool, Aldones.

Aldones: You should not have let them go.

Cassilda: *(Small.)* Now I have lost all of my children.

Aldones: I grieve with you, sister, I...

Cassilda: Oh, what do you know about grief? Who have you ever lost? Has anyone ever been close enough to you that you would notice their absence? You are cold as night, Aldones, cold as night. Do not pretend to sympathize or empathize with me, you who never cared for anything but my crown.

My child has died, damn you, and it's not some opportunity for comforting your coveted crown. I would give you the damned thing but for duty. I never wanted it. And now my son... my *sons* are dead and all you see is opportunity. Is there no shame in your cold heart, Aldones? None?

Aldones: (*Suddenly roused.*) What did he mean when he said there was a battle flag outside our gates? Has some rebel faction dared besiege us?

Naotalba: Perhaps it is the armies of the dead, come to claim the living.

Aldones: (*To Bicree.*) Tell Lieutenant Bilsh that he is in command now. Have him order the guard to go the gate. Assist the city watch. Let no one enter. Defend us.

Bicree: (*Salutes.*) Very good, my lord.

(EXIT Bicree. Scattered musket fire and shouts can now be heard in the distance. These are faint and occasional at first, but they grow in intensity and frequency, becoming at length quite loud, until Aldones fires.)

Aldones: The guard will deal with your friends, old man.

Naotalba: The end is foreordained.

Aldones: Shut up. We could shoot you here for treason.

Naotalba: The treason is yours. You tricked Camilla into signing the death warrant.

Aldones: *(To Cassilda.)* You see, sister? He as much as admits it. The only lie is the subject of it—the object remains true.

Naotalba: Lies!

Aldones: You tell them!

Cassilda: Gentlemen! Gentlemen, you bicker like children. Only Camilla knows the truth.

Aldones: And she's in the city, spreading priestly propaganda...

Cassilda: She's what?

Naotalba: She shows the Yellow Sign.

(A gong sounds. Cassilda sits up in her throne. The others peer about. ENTER Camilla. Her nightgown is dirty and torn; her hair is stringy and damp. She is holding the Stranger's robe tightly to her breast. Her gaze wanders until she sees Aldones. She smiles broadly, pauses a moment, and then dances around the room and waves the robe in the air like a flag.)

Naotalba: *(Wonderment.)* As if summoned, she appears.

Camilla: Great joy, uncle, for the Yellow Sign is found! Great joy to all who see it! Great...

Aldones: Traitor! You sell us to the priests and the mob! What price your treachery? What profit your crimes?

Camilla: *(Stops, uncertain and confused.)* Dear uncle...

Aldones: *(To Cassilda.)* It is a simple matter, your majesty. If she is mad, that's one thing. But if she simply acts

	of it, if she is indeed a traitor, then we must stop her.
Cassilda:	Your explanations wheel like a flight of sparrows, Aldones. I am growing impatient...
Naotalba:	*(To Cassilda.)* Her madness is a gift of the gods, for does she not speak truly?
Aldones:	Hardly.
Naotalba:	*(Ignoring Aldones.)* Did she not see Carcosa's rising tide?
Aldones:	No one sees it now, old man.
Naotalba:	*(To Aldones.)* She, like her brother before her, has dropped your dynasty's veil behind, So crossing from your destiny to mine.
Aldones:	So she's with you, then?
Naotalba:	Surely she has chosen madness wisely...
Aldones:	*(Shouting.)* Riddles, riddles! While war wages about us, ruin closer by the minute, you rhyme and preen and gloat! I've had enough!
Naotalba:	I am content to wait; the time cannot be long in coming.
Camilla:	But uncle, how is Uoht? I had him arrested...
Aldones:	*(Interrupting.)* The traitor admits it!
Camilla:	*(Overspoken by Aldones.)* ...as you asked me.
Cassilda:	Calm yourself, Aldones. She sounds to me as though her madness retreats a little, if such a thing were possible. Hear her out.

Aldones: If you will not defend our dynasty, I will!

Bremchas: There's nothing quite as heart-rending as a warm, freshly oiled muskrat...

(Aldones grabs the musket from Bremchas's hands and aims at Camilla.)

Bremchas: *(Annoyed.)* Hey!

Naotalba: *(Dives to the ground.)* Save us!

Cassilda: *(Stands and screams.)* No!

(Aldones fires. The musket flashes with fire and smoke, and Camilla crumples to the ground. As the explosive sound echoes away, absolute silence settles across the scene.)

Cassilda: *(Restrained and resigned.)* So. 'Tis true. 'Tis all true. After a fashion.

Aldones: *(Slightly stunned.)* Cassilda...

Cassilda: Only 'twas you. 'Twas you who sent Uoht to the tower, to his death. And now...

(Cassilda calmly draws her sword.)

Aldones: Dear sister!

Cassilda: To cover your lies...

Aldones: Not true!

Cassilda: *(Deliberately.)* Aldones. It is you who are the traitor.

(Aldones drops the musket, almost throwing it away. He shakes.)

Cassilda: You lied to me. You slack-brained piece of human filth. How long were you lying to me? How long? Just today? A week? A year? When have you not lied to me, to all of us?

Aldones: No! I... I... Naotalba. Yes, Naotalba...

Cassilda: *(Taking a step from the throne, growing in her anger as Aldones shrinks.)* What?

Aldones: He bewitched me.

Cassilda: *(Takes another step.)* Try again.

Aldones: I... I was mad.

Cassilda: *(Steps off of the dais.)* No.

Aldones: It's not my fault. I...

Cassilda: Draw your sword.

Aldones: But she was a... that is she... ah!

(Cassilda swings her sword at Aldones. Aldones backs away hurriedly and draws his sword; they fight. Aldones suffers several small wounds from Cassilda's vicious attacks. During the fight, Naotalba sits on the dais to watch. Bremchas soon joins him. He pulls a pear from his pocket and offers it to Naotalba, who refuses it.)

Cassilda: Murderer! Liar! *(She wounds him.)* You have destroyed us!

Aldones: I sacrificed the present... for the future.

Cassilda: Tell me—was it ambition or just a natural sense of cruelty that drove you? *(She wounds him.)*

(Aldones recovers his poise slightly and begins to fight back somewhat more effectively.)

Aldones: Destiny drove me.

Cassilda: Please...

Aldones: It was always my destiny to repudiate father's dismissal. You're such an idiot, Cassilda. You never had the will to do what was politically necessary.

(Aldones is again driven back by the ferocity of Cassilda's attack.)

Cassilda: *(Ever more emotional.)* Necessary? Necessary? What was necessary? Was Camilla necessary? Was Uoht *(She wounds him.)* necessary? My children; our future, that was your sacrifice, for your anger and your ego. Were all the *(She wounds him.)* murders necessary? The lies?

Aldones: *(Fear.)* Cassilda!

Cassilda: The torture—was that also politically necessary? or did you just *(She wounds him.)* enjoy it?

Aldones: Cassilda...

Cassilda: Why won't you die? *(She wounds him.)*

Aldones: I... I only wanted... to save us.

Cassilda: See how you have condemned us?

(Cassilda knocks Aldones's sword from his hand, and Aldones falls against the throne. Cassilda raises her sword for the killing blow and then—deus ex machina.)

(A gong sounds. The lights change suddenly to a reddish-purple. The banners flanking the throne fall, revealing banners emblazoned with the Yellow Sign. Bremchas and Naotalba stand in awe. Cassilda drops her sword. Aldones picks it up as he scrambles to his feet. The throne itself falls into the wall, and the wall begins to open up. Smoke issues from the gap. Cymbals clash, quietly at first, and then in accelerating crescendo, culminating in a deep gong. Yellow light fills the smoky hole where the throne was, and there stands the King in Yellow. Idiotic, soft random piping is heard until the darkness falls.)

(The King in Yellow is about three meters in height and is dressed in a scalloped and tattered hood and robe. His face is hidden by a roiling silken yellow veil. His hands are covered with yellow gloves. As He glides forward, his tatters flap in a sudden wind. He speaks with a deep, commanding voice. As He does so, a triangle keeps a measured beat.)

King: You have slain truth, and the old lies have triumphed. All shall achieve their desire at our court, but it shall avail them nothing.

Naotalba: *(To Cassilda.)* Do you see? Now do you see the truth? *(To Aldones, triumphantly.)* Your petty power struggles have availed you nothing! Now we shall...

King: *(Silences Naotalba with a wave, then points to Aldones.)* You desired a resurgence and extension of the empire; we say unto you that our empire is eternal, and you shall not see the end of it. Your dynasty has swallowed its children and shall not rule here again. Where has your rationality and certitude brought you?

(The King spreads wide his arms but a moment.)

Aldones: *(Shouting, sobbing, hacking with his sword wildly at the King, increasingly hysterical and incoherent.)* No!

No! It's mine! Mine! I won't be robbed again! I won't let you! It's mine!

(Aldones brandishes the sword and swings it at the King. The sword bounces off of the King and twists in Aldones's hands, causing him to strike himself. Aldones falls to the ground, dead.)

Bremchas: The rational and irrational are equally irrelevant. It's no good fighting the thief of destiny.

Naotalba: Show respect for your living god! *(Doubtfully.)* And he shall be merciful.

Bremchas: I'm too drunk to be polite. It's an uncomfortable truth of the universe that there are uncomfortable truths.

Naotalba: Of what use to him can I be?

Bremchas: The same we were to you, no doubt.

Naotalba: *(Frightened.)* Perhaps Prince Thale was right to flee?

Bremchas: Death's victory becomes a rout!

Naotalba: *(Begins to chant and creep away.)*
Oodás horasa mae,
gar esómí aorotos...

King: *(Suddenly points to Naotalba.)* You desired the commencement of a new age; we say unto you that we are the new age. Our reign has begun, but what need have we for priests when the eternal dead may serve us? Where has your irrationality and certitude brought you? Begone!

(The King spreads wide his arms but a moment. Naotalba screams and falls dead; a thick cloud of dust rises from his body.)

King: *(To Cassilda.)* You desired survival; we say unto you only that you have survived.

Cassilda: I have survived all of my children.

King: Was that not your desire? To survive? Or did we misunderstand?

Cassilda: But not like this! You've taken my children...

King: *(Interrupting.)* Not us. See where your conciliation and indifference have brought you?

Cassilda: *(Continues.)* ...but I shall not surrender. I shall never surrender. Thale may still live. He shall be the last king.

King: Thale was the *first* king. *We* are the Last King.

Cassilda: I shall not abdicate.

King: You already have.

(A pause.)

Cassilda: *(Small.)* Have you conquered Hastur then?

King: We *are* Hastur. We have reclaimed Yhtill from its human infestation. The parasites who continue to live here do so at our sufferance.

Cassilda: Is there nothing else?

King: How can you deny it?

Cassilda: *(Frantic.)* But surely Carcosa is your city, not Yhtill.

King: But now, this *is* Carcosa, for the doom of Carcosa is visited upon you all.

(The King spreads wide his arms.)

Cassilda: *(She collapses.)* Not upon us, oh King, not upon us!

(Sudden darkness, except for a single light upon Bremchas. Silence.)

Bremchas: *(Sadly.)* It is a fearful thing to fall into the hands of a living god.

(Darkness.)

(CURTAIN)

END

The Unseeing Eye

Ουδεις ορασα με,
γαρ εσομαι αοροτος
ως εξαφισταμαι
Καρκωσας.
Τρηχυαι ομιχηλαι
κρυπτει με,
και οστις αν
διερχονται
εσονται τυφλον.

None shall see me,
for I shall be invisible
as lost
Carcosa.
The tattered mists
shall hide me,
and those who pass
shall be
made blind.

Come.

"You are invited to a masquerade—
　The Palace, in the evening, one week hence,
　To celebrate the Birth-day of the Queen.
　Come in costume. Come to dine. Come to dance.
　But Come."

　　　　　You can't refuse the yellowed card.
With sad precision, all the guests arrive,
And you are greeted by the grinning guard
Who takes your coat and wonders at your mask.

Dance with the Princess of the empty eyes!
The Queen's cant is a dark delight, so sing!
And in the utter end the King appears
In the splendour of His decaying.

Hastur's the soul disease you've long suspected;
And in reading this, you've been infected.